Potter's Field 8

Novelettes
36 Beguiled by a Melancholy Knell by Lee Clark Zumpe
79 Good Magic by Katherine Kerestman

Short Stories
10 A Gift for the Dead by Christopher Langan
28 Necropolis by Paul Lonardo
60 The Call Stop by Kendra Preston Leonard
109 Self-Preservation by Lucretia Stanhope
121 The Haunting of Loon Lake by Tom Folske

Illustrations
59 Mourning the Nameless Ones by Amanda Bergloff

Poems
27 Forgotten by Kellee Kranendonk
35 Remonstrance by Patricia Gomes
78 April Shade by Patricia Gomes
   The Dead Have Ears by Greg Schwartz
108 Away From Home by Gary Davis
119 Hallow's Eve by Allison Liu
120 Haunted by K. S. Hardy

127 Who's Who?

*

THE STAFF OF HIRAETH PUBLISHING

MANAGING EDITOR: Tyree Campbell
WEBMASTER: H David Blalock
EDITOR: Christina Sng

Copyrights owned by the respective authors and artists
Cover art "The Forgotten" by Amanda Bergloff
Cover design by Laura Givens

All rights reserved. No part of this book may be reproduced or transmitted in any form or by any means, electronic or mechanical, including photocopying or recording or by any information storage and retrieval systems, without expressed written consent of the author and/or artists.
Potter's Field 8 is a work of fiction. Names, characters, places, and incidents are products of the author's imagination. Any resemblance to actual events or persons, living or dead, is entirely coincidental.

First Printing, July 2024

Hiraeth Publishing
P.O. Box 1248
Tularosa, NM 88352
e-mail: hiraethsubs@yahoo.com

Visit www.hiraethsff.com for online science fiction, fantasy, horror, scifaiku, and more. Stop by our online bookstore for novels, magazines, anthologies, and collections. **Support the small, independent press...and your First Amendment rights.**

A Little Help, Please

In the world of the small indie press we fight a never-ending battle for attention to our work, as writers and in publishing. Here's an example: big publishers [you know who they are] have gobs of $$$ that they can devote to advertising and marketing. Here at Hiraeth Publishing, our advertising budget consists of the deposits for whatever soda bottles and aluminum cans we can find alongside the highways. Anti-littering laws make our task even more difficult . . . ☺

That's where YOU come in. YOU are our best promoter. YOU are the one who can tell others about us. Just send 'em to our website, tell them about our store. That's all. Just that.

Of course, we don't mind if you talk us up. We're pretty good, you know. We have some award-winning and award-nominated writers and artists, plus other voices well-deserving to be heard [not everyone wins awards, right?] but our publications are read-worthy nevertheless.

That number once again is:
www.hiraethsffh.com

Friend us on Facebook at Hiraeth Publishing
Follow us on Twitter at @HiraethPublish1

Annae (real name Maryjade) is an assassin sent to Deege, a forested world, to kill a plant and bring back the druzy who carries it. Druzies resemble young girls, but seem to have no life and no purpose but to act as transportation to the plants. In the process, Annae loses contact with her own spacecraft and is marooned on the world.

The man who hired Annae for this task is also responsible for the death of Annae's twin sister. Annae has accepted this contract because it presents an opportunity to kill the killer. However, the loss of the twin has crippled Annae. She is virtually unable to communicate with anyone, except in the course of negotiating her contracts. She has taken to talking with the memory of her dead sister, and with no one else.

Now, marooned on Deege, she must find a way to break out of her isolation and communicate with the druzies, and with a strange young woman who cannot speak, or she will be compelled to remain on this world forever.

https://www.hiraethsffh.com/product-page/becoming-jade-by-tyree-campbell

parABnormal Magazine

H. David Blalock, ed
SUBSCRIPTIONS

parABnormal Magazine is a print digest [trade paperback format] released quarterly by Alban Lake Publishing, in March, June, September, and December. *ParABnormal* publishes original stories, articles, art, reviews, interviews, and poetry.

The subject matter of *parABnormal Magazine* is, yes, the paranormal. For us, this includes ghosts, spectres, haunts, various whisperers, and so forth. It also includes shapeshifters, mythological creatures, and creatures from various folklores. If your story also has science fiction or fantasy elements, we regard that as a plus.

1-year subscription:

https://www.hiraethsffh.com/product-page/parabnormal-magazine-subscription

Can You See Me?
By M. R. Williamson

After falling ill from a fever, Susan's parents put her in their car to go to the doctor. Along the way, a blowout causes the car to crash, killing the parents, who are unaware that their daughter had already died back at the house.

Every morning after the accident, Susan awakens in her upstairs bedroom to await the return of her parents. Time passes, and the house gains a spooky reputation that makes it almost impossible to sell. Prospective clients have been unable to cope with the mysterious goings-on . . . until now.

https://www.hiraethsffh.com/product-page/can-you-see-me-by-m-r-williamson

A Gift for The Dead
Christopher Langan

He doesn't want to go.

But Josie has always been the adventurous one. Plus, it isn't fair that she knows he can't say no to her.

"I promise you, it'll be fun!" The excitement from her smile lights up her half of the car.

"It doesn't sound like fun," he says for the tenth time.

Her eyes narrow but fail to subdue that infectious smile. "Do I detect *fear* coming from the Mighty Quinn?"

His fingers tense around the steering wheel and he tries not to sound like a six year old. "You know why I don't like graveyards. Plus, it feels... disrespectful."

Her laugh surprises him. "To who?"

"Their families."

Josie knows him well enough to understand that even though he's been griping the whole time, he won't turn the car around. They pass a modest chapel in silence and make their way further into the cemetery.

"Oh look," Josie says pointing out her window. "There's even fog!"

Quinn lets out a sigh as he slows the car to maneuver through the turns of the narrow road. "Fog? Really? Such a cliché. What other tropes are we going to run into? Is there a squeaky cast iron gate? Any demonic looking gargoyles in sight? I bet the groundskeeper is creepy as hell."

Josie smacks him in the arm. "I'm not in love with your tone right now."

He smiles and makes a show of massaging the spot she hit. "Okay, okay. I'll be good."

"You'd better be, Mister. Otherwise, spankings will commence."

"Threaten me with a good time," Quinn says with a demure glance.

Her eyelids close halfway and she leans in for a quick kiss, to which he happily obliges.

The graveyard isn't what they expected. Although there is a layer of gloomy fog, there are no dilapidated tombstones overgrown with unholy vines. Nor are there trees with gnarled, drooping branches reaching to snatch the souls from their bodies.

Instead, it feels like cruising through a lovely, gated park. Through the thin layer of low fog, the couple catches glimpses of evenly spaced depressions where bronze headstones lay flat against the hallowed earth. It looks as if buttons are pushing down into a massive cushion of soil. The thought of the dead finding eternal rest in a comfortable place adds a tranquil peace to the night. Although, Quinn feels a pang of sorrow course through him as he notices precious few flowers scattered among the grave markers.

"Are you sure this is the right graveyard?"

Josie crumples her lips to one side of her mouth. "The clips said it would be spooky here."

"The clips? Josie... are we chasing another social media trend?"

She frowns, but there's no real anger behind it. "Hey, several top influencers said this was the best place for a spooky experience. Maybe the groundskeeper can point us in the right direction?"

They look out as far as the fog allows. In the distance, haloed discs of light appear to hover in formation. As they approach, the discs materialize into a casually lit building.

The single story home is smaller than the attached garage. It looks to have two rooms—three if they're small. 'Shack' is a good word to describe the structure. Four different landscaping vehicles in various states of disrepair are parked on what some might consider a front yard. A deflated tractor tire leans against the home, while an honest to goodness outhouse stands guard in the backyard.

"Glad I went to the bathroom before we left," Quinn mumbles as he parks the car along the curb.

"Yeah, I'm with you on that one," Josie agrees. "C'mon, let's go."

Quinn opens his mouth to complain about how late it is, and that they should not disturb the groundskeeper, but the words die in his throat as the splintered door creaks open. An ancient man with a wispy gray beard steps on to the porch. His thin coat frays at the elbows and around the lower seams. The tweed golf cap above his brow looks as if it's spent more time in the dirt than on his head.

Quinn snorts. "He's not creepy, just old."

Undeterred, Josie exits the car before Quinn kills the engine. She bounces excitedly up to the man. "Hi there! We're here for—"

"Twenty-five bucks," he says. "Thirty if you want a guide."

Josie cocks her head to the side, then looks back at Quinn questioningly. With hands resting on the roof of the car, he stands next to the open driver's side door.

He shrugs. "That doesn't sound too—"

"A piece," the groundskeeper says loud enough for both of them to hear.

Quinn frowns. "A piece? That's a little steep for—"

"Price goes up to fifty after midnight," the man says.

Quinn checks his watch. 11:54 pm. Josie is waiting for an answer with a look on her face that he has no defense against.

"Ok, fine. Where should I—"

"Leave your car there." The man shuts the door to his home, then faces them with an expectant look.

Quinn smirks. "Not much for letting people finish a sentence, are ya?"

The groundskeeper says nothing and maintains his gaze. Neither of them can tell if he's annoyed or indifferent.

With a sigh, Quinn pulls out his wallet and delivers two twenties and a ten. Josie would love a tour, but something beyond the keeper's outgoing personality doesn't sit right. And Quinn wasn't about to go against his gut feeling. Not when it's served him so well.

The groundskeeper palms the cash and turns to head off into the dark of the graveyard. After locking the car, Quinn follows Josie as she skips her way over the trimmed grass.

With a handful of quick steps, he catches up to Josie who has taken a flanking position to the groundskeeper's right. She locks her arm in Quinn's with a giggle and a smile.

"This is going to be great," she says with a mile-wide grin. "Thank you, Babe."

Any annoyance he has about the price or the ethical implications of using the dead for a cheap thrill melts away, and he returns a smile filled with genuine happiness. "Making you happy makes me happy."

She squeezes his arm tighter and leans her head on his shoulder as they follow the groundskeeper. He leads them back along the winding road towards a modest stone fountain at the center of the graveyard. Solemn angels stand above a water-filled base while a few submerged coins litter the bottom.

The keeper stops and turns. "Start here. Come back to your car when you're done."

The couple nods.

His face takes on an unusual look. It feels predatory for a moment, then it doesn't. "Do not go into the gated section."

Josie frowns at the restriction. "Why not?"

"Because it's off limits."

The two of them share a glance. Josie purses her lips and shrugs. "Okay."

Quinn recognizes the meaning behind her response along with a sinking feeling in his stomach.

The keeper eyes them for a moment. It feels awkward, like he's trying to figure out if he could take them in a fight. He easily has thirty years on them and that's being generous. Even with his oversized coat, it's obvious he moves with a deliberate slowness that occasionally comes with age. Yet, his stare belies something deeper. Quinn can't tell if it's sinister, but his gut tells him to tread carefully.

Josie senses the pause but reaches a different conclusion. "Thank you," she says sheepishly.

"Yes," Quinn adds, "thank you."

The keeper's stare lingers for a moment longer, then with a grunt he walks back in the direction of his shack.

Josie grabs Quinn's hand and smiles. "Are you ready?"

He grins despite the coming unpleasantness. "Yeah."

She pulls out a folded sheet of paper and they start walking. With determined focus, she starts comparing the names on the paper to the names on the headstones. They take extra care not to step on any of the graves.

Josie and Quinn spend an hour walking up and down the rows of headstones, all the while checking names against the list. Josie's frustration grows as they scour the premises without finding a single name. Even a search of the crematorium yields no results.

"Ugh," she says. "There are fifty-five names on my list and we haven't found any of them."

"Maybe they were moved?"

"No, I checked before we left. They should be here," she says. A familiar look of mischief blossoms on her face. "You know, there is one place we haven't looked yet."

"Groundskeeper said it was off limits."

"Yeah, I know," she says. "But it's not against the law, right? Not like we're trespassing. We paid to be here."

"We really shouldn't."

Quinn watches as the defeat consumes her being. "Okay," she says. "We can go."

Josie isn't the type to use guilt to manipulate someone, but Quinn feels it anyway. "Tell you what, why don't I do a random one?"

Her frown melts away. "You'd do that for me?"

He takes her hands in his. "Of course, I would."

Her eyes water through an irresistible smile. "Thank you."

She leads him a handful of paces to the nearest headstone, taking care not to step directly over the prominent low mound.

From the side, they read the particulars: Janet Corsovich. Born April 2nd, 1963. Died August 7th, 2015. Loving mother, wife, and friend.

"She was, what? Fifty-two years old? Could be interesting," Josie says, studying the bronze engraving.

"Yeah."

She releases Quinn's hand and takes a step back. Her expectant smile fills his heart.

Quinn takes a deep breath and steps on to the grave. His eyes roll back into his head.

The cemetery evaporates and is replaced by the broken interior of a car. Quinn can't see much beyond the spider web pattern of the mangled windshield but he can tell the ground is not where it should be. He tries to look around but his head is pinned down by the crumpled roof. Pain radiates from everywhere except his legs. He feels the life draining out of his body.

Behind his head, he hears a young voice crying.

Reaching his limit, he blinks three times and the nightmare ends.

He's back in the graveyard. Instinctively, he hops to the side so that he is no longer standing on the grave.

Josie eyes her boyfriend with a familiar eagerness. "What did you see this time?"

Quinn shakes his arms out, relishing the absence of pain. "Car crash. Pretty bad."

Josie deflates. "Ah. Sorry. I know those are particularly rough for you."

"Yeah." He doesn't tell her about the crying kid and she knows not to ask.

He forces a smile. "Shall we try another?"

She sees through the façade. "No. We should go. The random ones are too rough on you."

Josie turns in the direction of the car and takes a few steps.

Quinn sighs. "Wait. How many do you think we could get done in the restricted area before the keeper kicks us out?"

The smile on her face is bright enough to make him forget that it's the dead of night.

The gated area is more in line with the type of graveyard seen in a horror movie. Twisted iron bars shoot skyward and curl into devilish thorns. The gate itself is fastened to a high brick wall in need of repairs. Two bronze seals depict branches of fruit and a setting sun.

"No crosses or anything," Josie notes.

"Is that a good sign?"

She shrugs excitedly. "Beats me. Let's go find out."

A hopeful thought strikes him. "What if it's locked?"

Josie steps up to the gate and pushes. The iron squeals in protest, but swings open with little effort.

"It's not," she says impishly.

"Wonderful."

Josie steps through the gate and gasps. While the main graveyard is a prairie of bronze headstones, the forbidden area is a metropolitan skyline of tombstones and statues. A few are simple granite, but most are works of incredible gothic art. Life-size angels spread intricate wings while towering scenes replicate famous works of religious iconography. Quinn recognizes The Last Supper and The Creation of Adam. Others look familiar, but morbid curiosity hampers his recall.

"Whoa," Quinn says with genuine awe.

Josie moves with reverence among the sculptures. "Now this is more like it."

He follows as she meanders through the forbidden area, happy to let her wander instead of performing his unique ability.

After a handful of minutes, she spreads her arms in confusion.

"None of these have names."

Quinn frowns and looks to the nearest grave. "All this elaborate artwork for unmarked graves? I don't get it."

"Maybe they were soldiers or something?" she says, scanning the base of an ornate sculpture of the Virgin Mary.

Quinn scratches his head. "As far as I know, there's only one unmarked grave for a soldier and that's more of a symbolic thing."

They keep walking as angels and cherubs look down. Quinn notices that all of the faces are twisted in agony. Stone tears leak from downturned eyes. It's enough to make him shiver.

"I've got something," Josie squeals with excitement. "Still no name, but there's an inscription. 'May God have mercy on your soul.'"

"That doesn't sound good," he says, "but now I'm curious."

Josie pats him on the shoulder. "That's the spirit! Now get in there and see what there is to see."

Quinn steps on to the raised patch of grass and his eyes roll back.

He squints against an overwhelming brightness. After a moment of recovery, he can tell that he is looking out of a second story window into a sunny, countryside front yard.

Curiously, there is no pain in this body. Flashing lights draw their attention to the horizon where they can see a line of police cars approaching at high speed.

Ah. It's one of these, *Quinn thinks to himself.*

Sure enough, the person he's onboard with turns around to a gruesome scene. A scantily clad woman is laying on a bed. Her face is frozen in terror and three dark holes mar the skin of her abdomen.

That's when Quinn feels the gun in their hand.

They don't move as the sirens close in on the house. No doubt the murderer is trying to figure out how to get out of this alive.

A whisper from the closet catches their attention. They walk over and fling the door open. A naked man is cowering in the corner. He is mumbling into a cell phone pressed against his ear. His eyes turn into saucers at the sight of them.

"Oh God! He found me! He has a gun!"

Their hand raises and they fire three shots into the closet. As always, Quinn is powerless to alter the events. The naked man drops the phone and slumps to the floor.

The sirens are much closer now. They walk back to the window and see that the cop cars have taken up a perimeter. Officers stand behind open doors with their weapons trained on the house.

A man points a bullhorn at the window. "Des Moines PD! Come out with your hands up!"

They lean out the window and shout. "I can't go back to prison! I won't!"

"You're surrounded! Give it up, Quinn!"

The world slows and Quinn's mind turns to sludge. That's not possible.

The officer lowers his bullhorn and speaks in a deep whisper that shouldn't be able to reach his ears. "Oh, I'm afraid it is very possible, Quinn."

He blinks his eyes three times.

Back in the graveyard, Josie sees the panic on Quinn's face before he can readjust to the change in environment.

"What happened?"

He frantically scans for approaching danger, but all he can see are elaborate tombstones.

"Something is *very* wrong. We have to get out of here."

Josie pulls out her phone. "What is it? Should I call for help?"

"No. It's my gift," he says hurriedly. "I only ever watch, but this time someone talked to me. C'mon!"

Josie's face goes pale as Quinn grabs her hand and leads her to the iron gate. "Someone *spoke* to you?"

"Yes," he says, stepping over the cursed graves.

"What did they say?"

"They called me by name," he says, "right before they were about to die in a police shootout."

Josie gasps. "Oh my God. Quinn, what if all of these unmarked graves are filled with murderers? And one of them knows your name..."

"I don't think it was just one," he says as he leads her through the labyrinth of footpaths.

"What do you mean?"

Quinn wipes the sweat from his brow. "I don't know. It's hard to describe, but it felt like there was more than just one of them in there with me. Like a large crowd speaking in unison."

Ten yards from the gate, a familiar figure appears. The groundskeeper stands just beyond the threshold.

Relief washes over them. Before Quinn can shout, he feels Josie's hand slip away. He keeps his open, thinking that she will grab it again. When she doesn't, he turns around.

Josie is standing motionless with her foot grazing the edge of disturbed earth. Her eyes are rolled back in her head.

"Josie!"

She doesn't have the gift. She shouldn't be able to relive the death of anyone. But they have her. Whoever, or whatever they are, knew Quinn's name and was able to take her from him.

Josie reaches out with curled fingers. "Take my hand, Babe."

Quinn takes several backwards steps, his gaze fixed on the pure white of her eyes. "No. Leave her alone! She doesn't have the gift!"

The entity controlling Josie cocked her head to the side. "No. But you do. Join us."

Quinn reels around to face the groundskeeper. "Help me! How do I free her?"

His pleas are met with a slow shake of the old man's head. "I told you this place was off limits. But I guess that's what lures people in the most. That, and the fancy tombstones."

Quinn shakes his head in confusion. "What in the hell are you talking about?"

For the first time, the groundskeeper smiles. It lacks anything close to joy or happiness and instills the deepest dread he's ever felt.

"You'll see."

Quinn's nostrils flare as he feels the first embers of anger. He takes a deep breath and returns his attention to Josie.

Get mad later, he tells himself. *Save Josie now.*

He surveys the scene and considers his options. Every solution more than likely results with both of them getting trapped by the entity in the death vision. Quinn knows it can't do much without physical contact but to what degree? Can it get him if he gets too close? It goes through clothing, as illustrated by Josie's shoe touching the grave, but is there a material that could insulate him? Maybe he could throw something at her to knock her foot away from the mound.

Quinn looks for something he can throw but all he sees are soulless angels and everlasting stone. He'd throw his shoe, but that wouldn't be enough to move her.

A desperate thought runs through his mind.

Quinn takes a few steps away from his frozen mate and squares his shoulders. He aligns himself to get the best possible angle. Then he charges.

Knowing it won't take much to move her, he keeps his speed relatively slow. At the last few steps, he goes low and aims his shoulders at her waist. On the final step, he extends his arms and lifts up.

There is a brief flash of...something. Water? A boat? Then his feet are off the ground and Josie's in his arms. He is desperate to keep them both out of the death visions, but they land squarely on the adjacent grave and his eyes roll back into his head.

He finds himself strapped to a chair in a concrete room. The taste of rubber fills his mouth and leather straps dig into his wrists. He can't exactly tell what's on the top of his head but he has a pretty good guess.

A glass window separates Quinn and the owner of the vision from a small crowd. Most are wearing business casual attire, while a few law enforcement officers stand in the rear. Notably, a priest is present. To their right is an unnatural mirror image of their execution. Every movement of every person in the room is mimicked in the reflection. The only difference is a woman bound to a similar chair looking back at them. It's Josie.

Her voice is as near panic as one can get. "Quinn! What is happening?"

Before he can answer, the observers on both sides of the reflection speak with a dissonant wave of a thousand voices. "Quinn... Josie... stay with us. Quinn... Josie... stay with us."

He shouts so Josie can hear him above the monotonous chanting. "Blink three times!"

She frowns as the chanting gets louder. "What?"

"Blink three times!"

The unholy cacophony fills both versions of the room. It's loud enough to rattle Quinn's sternum.

"BLINK! THREE! TIMES!"

Her face goes blank for a moment, then her eyes flutter. Her head rolls to the side and the mirror image evaporates, leaving behind the fourth wall of the room.

As soon as she gets out, the air grows thick and a wave of dizziness assaults Quinn's consciousness.

The voices grow louder than what he knows to be possible. "QUINN! JOIN US!"

The voices wail inside his head. He feels himself drifting towards madness. "You have a gift, Quinn. An incredible gift. Join us and you can live forever."

"This isn't living," he growls.

Fighting through the mental fog, he blinks three times.

He finds himself back in the graveyard. Reflexively, he jumps to the isle where the dead cannot reach. Josie stands on the same path with her back to him. Relief fills his soul knowing she's safe from whatever unholy entity is pursuing them.

"Josie!" Quinn takes a few steps towards her. "We gotta get out of here. Whatever you do, don't step on the graves. They only have power in the death visions."

Dread and sorrow weigh him down as the woman he loves slowly turns around. Despite standing in the safety of the footpath, he can only see the whites of her eyes.

A menacing smile spreads across her face as she speaks with many voices. "We have power here too, Quinn."

Thoughts of escape flash through his mind. In an optimistic scenario, he flees the graveyard and returns with the police to rescue Josie. But he knows that is pure fantasy.

Josie takes a few deliberate steps toward him. He can hear the other, darker, voices beneath hers when she speaks. "My Mighty Quinn. We really should stay. It is so much more exciting than anything outside these walls.

With your gift, we can extend our influence and offer paradise to many more souls. C'mon, Babe. Let's spend eternity together."

Quinn tries to swallow the lump in his throat but it doesn't budge. "They're murderers. Monsters. Every last one of them in this little corner of hell. Fight them, my love. Push them out of your mind."

Her shoulders twitch at his words. Her head jerks from side to side and causes her ponytail to brush against her forehead. The convulsions never reach her legs allowing the internal battle to rage without sending her body to the ground.

After an agonizing moment, her muscles relax and she looks at Quinn with despair and longing.

A tear emerges from the corner of her eye. "I'm sorry, Babe. They're too...strong. Don't...let me...touch...you..."

Once again, he faces the piercing white of an unnatural gaze.

The entities controlling Josie are done talking. She lunges with arms fully extended.

Skirting the edge of the footpath, he barely manages a quick sidestep that takes his feet dangerously close to a grave. He leans backwards as far as he dares in order to dodge Josie's attack.

The gambit works. She sails by, her hands coming within inches of grabbing his shirt. He takes several instinctive steps in the other direction as she crashes on the ground behind him.

Josie recovers quickly and stands ready to try again. Quinn's heart sinks when he realizes her leap has placed her on the footpath between him and the exit.

He takes off at a full sprint in the opposite direction. A double vocal laugh bounces an echo behind him. His eyes dart frantically, looking for any avenue of escape.

The far wall of the closed off area looms about forty yards ahead. There is no visible door or gate. Quinn glances to his left and right, hoping to see another way out, but his line of sight is blocked by the stone monuments of fiends.

The path breaks off into three directions when it meets the wall. Keeping his hurried steps on the path of safety, he leans into a hard right turn and continues to flee.

Josie surprisingly shouts with a multi-layered voice from close behind. "There's no way out. Might as well stay a bit!"

Quinn risks a glance over his shoulder and see that he's in far more danger than he realizes. Josie has always been more or less his athletic equal, so he hopes that he can at least maintain his lead. He fails to take into account that his gift limits him to the footpath, while her forced immunity lets her run over any grave she wishes. So, while his only choice is to follow the approaching ninety-degree turn, Josie is free to run across graves. The sound of her rapidly approaching shoes is dreadful in his ears.

His legs pump as fast as they ever have while his breathing fights to keep up.

Think! His thoughts go to his phone, but he would lose too much speed and concentration while trying to remove it from his pocket. He considers throwing it at her but quickly realizes it would make a poor weapon.

Like its counterpart, the path he's running on leads to another wall. He looks for another intersection, but only sees rows of towering tombstones. At the last second, a narrow path appears, running along the edge of the wall.

Leaping over the corner of the last grave, his feet land too close to the wall. He stumbles and cries out as his shoulder hits the ancient bricks. The impact spins him around and his legs threaten to buckle. Whether by luck or divine intervention, he is miraculously able to stay upright and continue running.

Quinn steals another glance over his shoulder, only to see Josie reaching out to grab him.

Panic supercharges his legs as he pours on more speed than he thought was possible. Josie's outstretched hand catches nothing but air. The effort of the lunge throws her off balance. She flails her arms and takes slow, extended steps to recover. The action keeps her from falling but allows Quinn to put some distance between them.

Empowered by good fortune, he keeps running. Josie continues her pursuit but isn't able to make any significant gains. He knows if he can just make it to the corner, he'll have a clear path to the exit.

Quinn checks again to make sure his possessed beloved hasn't gotten any closer.

She's gone.

For a fleeting moment, he pictures her giving up the chase. Then he looks to his right and sees her running across the low mounds, turning and ducking past the opulent statues to cut him off. Though she's increasing her distance, they both know there is only one exit.

And she's going to beat him to it.

For lack of a better plan, he rounds the corner anyway and races toward the iron gate. Again, there is a path separating the wall from a row of tightly packed graves. Midway to the opposing side, he can see the darkened iron bars of the open gate. It's about thirty or forty yards away.

Quinn loses sight of Josie among the fog and the forest of sculptures, but still keeps an eye on his right. The sound of her pursuit fades, making way for the thunderous pounding of his heart. He runs, not knowing how he will deal with her or with any of this.

With a victorious shout, she appears directly in front of him. At full speed, he resists the urge to plant his heels knowing it would still result in a collision. Instead, he jumps directly toward a grave. His hope is that momentum will carry him across several graves and break the entity's concentration just enough for him to get back on the footpath.

It's a plan hanging by a thin string of hope, but it's all he's got. He takes a breath as Josie's hand misses his knee and his foot lands on a grave...

Quinn appears in another concrete room. An IV is attached to his arm and familiar leather straps restrain his movement. Voices call from the audience in the next room.

"At last! Welcome to your new—"

He blinks three times before the entities can react.

...Quinn's other foot lands and his arms flail. He brings them in and try to shift his weight back to the path. Momentum forces him to take an involuntary step on the next grave...

His hands are tied behind his back. He's secured against a wooden post. Dust cakes his mouth. A line of men with rifles glare at him in the sweltering sun.
The voices call out. "It won't make any difference."
Quinn blinks three times.

...He takes another step and makes another shift. He can feel his body heading back in the right direction...

Another concrete room with him in an electric chair. The voices are getting agitated.
"Stop this!"
He blinks twice. There is a slight upwards pull on the third blink.

...Quinn stretches his left leg and re-establishes contact with the footpath. But loose gravel slides under his shoe and brings him down. His hip lands hard on the forgiving grass of the next grave...

A crowd of people wearing old-looking clothes is staring at him. Quinn is standing on a wooden platform with a rope around his neck.
The voices are almost pleading. "Stay with us! Live forever!"
He blinks twice. A force fights against his eyelids to keep them from closing a third time. He strains and struggles only to close them halfway before they open again.
The voices take on a sinister tone. "We win in the end. We always do."

...He's on his back, looking at a starless sky. He props himself up and sees that he is on the footpath. The ploy seems to have worked. The iron gate is mere feet away. He can see out into the main cemetery through the clearing fog. The groundskeeper is nowhere in sight.

"Quinn?" Josie's voice is singular and pure. "Babe, it's time to stop." There is no ethereal echo or any indication that anyone else is speaking. Her eyes are the dark brown heartbreakers he originally fell for. It's just her. For whatever reason, the entities are letting her speak to Quinn. Perhaps for the last time.

"No," he says with a quivering voice. "Whatever they promised, it's a lie. They're evil, Josie. I've seen the lives they've ended. They're monsters and they want me for my gift."

She sighs. "It's not all that bad. All the things I love, the spookiness, the macabre, everything that's considered weird, all of that is normal for them. For the first time in my life, I can be *me*. The true me. The me I started being when I was around you. The only thing missing is you, my love. Come with us. Come with me."

Josie easily closes the distance before he can even think about standing up. Her hand caresses his shoulder.

Josie has always been the adventurous one.

But he doesn't want to go.

Forgotten
Kellee Kranendonk

Lost and forgotten on top of a hill
Headstones peek through the numerous ferns
The spirits they rise, reach for the sky
Separate from bones, leave them behind.

Ethereal beings call from the grave
Spread out their vibes, confine me until
I promise them hope, their memories to bring
Back to the moment, the present and more.

They desire remembrance, and that isn't all
Some secrets are hidden, but that shouldn't be
They ask me to look, seek the truth out
What ancient bones lay insulted and injured?

Black clouds roll in and thunder, it crashes
The lightning lights up a deep weedy gulch
What's down there that's stuck, entombed all alone
With no sign, no justice, no home.

Rain starts to sprinkle, slides between leaves
But this feeling won't leave me, I can't get away
Chilly chalk fingers run down my spine
In silence the voices, call from their graves.

I must right this wrong, this ancient injustice
I've been tasked with an otherworldly request
I promise to free the oldest of souls, to unearth
The bones that cry out in silence

A silence that I have heard on this night
That screamed in my head and ignited a passion
The rain soaks my skin, the pleas soak my soul
But I will return to fulfill my calling

Necropolis
Paul Lonardo

Existence in this retirement community was pure monotony. Even for Adam, a former schoolteacher who has always believed in the importance of structure to help a person remain on track mentally and physically, the tedium of this place had grown unbearable. Every day was the same, except perhaps for Wednesday mornings when the men in the brown coveralls showed up to cut the grass. They'd come riding on the backs of oversized power mowers and trundling along with grass trimmers in hand. However, even this distraction was part of the dreary reality at Shady Hollow.

Adam thought the landscape maintenance must have been included in the price of the unit because he never paid an additional fee for the service.

He would come outside all the time to watch the men work. There wasn't much else for him to do. Besides, the men made enough noise to wake the dead with the collective engine roar of all their machines. They never said a word to him. They were so focused on their work that they didn't even look at him as they silently and efficiently did their jobs while listening to music only they could hear thrumming through the tiny speakers in their airbuds.

The men would zip through all the units on the street like they were racing against the clock, churning up clouds of dirt and pollen into the air before moving on to the other units in the development, which stretched out far and wide in every direction, well beyond the range of what Adam's tired, old eyes could see.

Indeed, Shady Hollow was a massive community, built in phases over time. It had been well established by the time Adam arrived, which even though the exact date escaped him, it didn't seem all that long ago.

Funny, I can't seem to remember when I moved in, he thought. *Oh, well, what difference does it make? I'm here now and I'm not going anywhere.*

One thing he did know, there were a lot of retirees in this community, some of whom had been there a long time. Whoever owns this piece of land must be stinking rich, he figured, because the place was constantly expanding as more and more people moved in. There was some freshly broken ground just around the corner from him in a section where a young forest full of aspens, maples, and birches once stood. They had taken away all the trees, and with them went the shade and privacy they had provided, and there were all new units on that spot now.

That's progress, Adam supposed. What can you do? But at least he'd have new neighbors soon. He was looking forward to that. He didn't even know his neighbors on either side. He couldn't recall ever meeting them. They were probably really old, he thought, and slept a lot. Boredom could do that to a person. He understood that, and that's why he would go out as much as possible, if only to stretch his legs a little, see another soul once in a while.

It seemed the only time he saw anybody was when they first moved in. They always looked around with confused and alarmed expressions on their faces, like they didn't want to be there. Adam tried to tell them it wasn't that bad there, and that they'd get used to it, it just takes a little time. He didn't think he managed to convince any of them, however. After the first day, he didn't see them again. They never came outside, so it was hard to remember what they even looked like.

There was one person, he remembered, who came out every day from sunup to sundown for about a week. It was a teenage boy, high school age. He was a good distance from Adam, atop a high slope, but Adam had a clear view of him. He was a big kid. He wore a brand-new pair of jeans and a high school football jersey with the number "8" on the back. He had only white socks on his feet. Adam figured the kid was there visiting his grandparents, but it became obvious rather quickly that he was lost. He'd pace around nervously, calling for his mother repeatedly. He'd stop for a little while, and Adam could hear him crying. Then the kid would continue calling for his mother. Adam felt terrible. No one seemed to want to help him.

Adam wanted to do something himself, but he didn't know what. In some ways, he felt a lot like the kid did. Adam didn't really want to be there either. He was starting to get the feeling that nobody wanted to be there.

Anyway, after a few days, just like everyone else, the kid was gone. Adam hadn't seen him since and didn't know what happened to him. Adam liked to believe that the kid had been reunited with his mother, or maybe someone else had come for him. He hoped so, because this was no place for someone that young, unless they *were* visiting their grandparents.

The men in the brown coveralls were the only ones who seemed truly at ease there. When they were not cutting and trimming the grass, they did other work at Shady Hollow. In the spring, they came to clear away the twigs and other debris that accumulated around the units over the winter. In the fall they'd rake the leaves that had dropped from the scattering of maple and oak trees that still remained. Some mornings they'd come and plant flowers at the front of some of the units, oddly, even in the winter when there was snow on the ground. They always smelled so good. Adam liked to come out to enjoy the fragrant scent. Roses were a particular favorite. On Mother's Day, they were everywhere. The powdery, fruity aroma would waft through the community from every direction. But Easter was the very best with the abundance of bouquets, the bright pastel colors, the calla lilies and the daffodils. Poinsettias and Hollies at Christmastime were nice, too. However, what was so frustrating was that the flowers were not there for very long. They never got any water unless it rained, and if they didn't wither and die in the hot sun first, the men would come and rip them out after only a week. The men who planted and removed the flowers came at all hours of the day, often when Adam was sleeping. He'd been napping a lot since he retired and moved there, but a few times he came out and caught them taking the flowers away. He yelled at them, but they just ignored him, acting like he wasn't even there. Adam had a good mind to complain, but he didn't know who to complain to.

Occasionally some of the older units were adorned with artificial flowers. They usually remained in place longer than the real flowers because they didn't require any care. But eventually they'd get discolored and moldy and were removed, too.

The units on Adam's street were all the same size, same shape, built of the same solid stone, which certainly helped to keep him cool in the summer. There were units in other parts of the development that varied quite a bit in terms of dimension and architectural design. Off in the far distance were virtual mansions with grandiose gothic features; pointed arches, gargoyles, and spires that reached up toward the heavens. They were visible from anywhere in the development. These were massive structures, some so immense it made Adam wonder why anyone would build such a monolith when something less extravagant would serve the same purpose.

Why not? Adam thought. *Some people can afford it. If you got it, you may as well spend it. You can't take it with you, as the old saying goes.*

There were also sections where people of lesser means resided. Their units were modest, much smaller than Adam's. He felt a little sad for them. No one would ever confuse him for someone who was rich, but to the people who lived in that particular section of the community, maybe he was rich. It was just nice that everyone had somewhere to go in the end.

Adam hadn't gotten around to visiting any of these sections of Shady Hollow yet. Maybe he would someday, he didn't know. There was no point, really.

Looking around now, he realized that he was not alone. One of his neighbors was out. A woman. She was lying down, completely reclined on her back, staring up at the blue sky and the thin veil of clouds that wandered by intermittently.

Thinking she might be unwell, or injured and in need of help, Adam asked, "Are you okay?"

She didn't react right away, then suddenly she raised her torso off the ground. She remained in a sitting position and looking straight ahead. She was wearing a floral print gown with long sleeves and a high neckline. A gentle breeze ruffled the tail of her bright purple scarf behind her. She seemed overdressed for such a warm early June morning. Although she was wearing a lot of makeup, she looked familiar, her short hair colored amber and set in thick curls.

As she slowly swiveled her head in his direction, he realized where he'd seen her before.

She was his wife, Barbara.

Why is she living next door to me?

Adam shuddered involuntarily as a feeling of dread and unease washed over him.

"Barbara?" His voice trembled. He couldn't remember the last time he spoke her name. "What are you doing over there?"

Her face was set in a permanent smile. Just under the surface, however, a forlorn expression foretold a darker truth.

"Why aren't you here with me?" He tried to walk over to her, but he found that his ability to move was restricted, his legs bound in place.

He heard the drone of gas-powered engines revving up in the distance and realized it must be Wednesday.

"Barbara, say something." Adam noticed that his wife's eyes were closed. They appeared sealed shut. Her lips, as well. He could see dried glue crusted in the corners.

The men in the brown coveralls headed down the street. The riding movers came through in the first wave, followed by the men with the power trimmers. The ones with the backpack blowers were last.

"BARBARA," he yelled over the sound of the engine noise and whirring blades. WHAT'S HAPPENING?"

She just shook her head. She couldn't speak and Adam could not reach her even though they were only separated by a couple of feet.

None of this made any sense to Adam, and from the anguished cast to Barbara's face, he could tell that she could read the profound exasperation in my voice. He recalled the teenage boy crying and calling for his mother, imagining how alone he must have felt.

"There's something wrong," Adam said, his voice growing weaker. "I don't understand this."

With her head tilted to one side in despair, she raised her finger and pointed at something behind him. Whatever she was trying to indicate, she was doing so with such reluctance that Adam knew it could not be anything pleasing. Part of him didn't want to look, but he turned slowly toward his unit, not knowing what to expect. At first, he saw only what he wanted to see, a simple dwelling made of whitewashed stone, one of many just like it all around him.

"What is it?" he fumed softly. "I don't know what you want me to see."

Then he saw it.

ADAM W. GABLINSKI.

His name, in clear Romanesque calligraphy, was carved into the stone. Beneath that, LOVING FATHER AND DEVOTED HUSBAND OF BARBARA GABLINSKI. There were two dates in a smaller font near the bottom, FEBRUARY 12, 1940 – JUNE 4, 2023. The first date was his birthday.

Adam heard an audible gasp, his own. He snapped his head back around toward Barbara, but she was gone, and the only thing he saw was another grave marker with the epitaph:

IN EVERLOVING MEMORY
BARBARA GABLINSKI
WIFE, MOTHER, SOUL MATE
NOVEMBER 12, 1945 – MAY 7, 2023

"No, no, no, no, no!" he screamed, thinking that he could deny reality the louder and longer he screamed.

***

"Okay, Joe, that takes care of this section," said one landscaper seated on a commercial lawn mower to another one carrying a gasoline-powered grass trimmer. "We'll meet you and your guys at the next section when you're done here." He spoke loudly, with both his hands cupped around his mouth to replicate the effect of a bull horn.

Joe, shirtless and wearing earbuds, acknowledged his crew boss with a thumbs up.

"And Joe, be sure you trim around the headstones extremely carefully in this section. Some of the families are complaining that the stones are being damaged by the trimmer lines. These people paid a lot of money for those markers, so take your time and be extra cautious."

Nooooooooo!

Joe switched off his trimmer and pulled his earbuds out. He stood perfectly still, his face pinched in wonder and his head tilted to one side.

His crew boss sidled up beside him, dropping his safety earmuffs down around his neck. "What's wrong?"

"Did you hear that?" Joe asked.

"Hear what?"

"I don't know. It sounded like a scream."

"You're hearing things again," the crew boss scoffed. He was much older than Joe, and unlike Joe, every inch of his skin was protected from the sun. He had on gray sweatpants, a long-sleeve white hooded sweatshirt that he was already starting to sweat through, and a wide brimmed safari hat with a neck shield,

"I swear I heard it," Joe professed with a nervous smile.

"Just get back to work," the crew boss told him as he pulled his ear protection back up atop his head. "And go easy around those stones."

Joe waited until his crew boss was gone and it was relatively quiet. He listened keenly for any sound, but he didn't hear a thing. He glanced over at the gravestone behind him.

ADAM GABLINSKI.

Then he realized that the gravestone beside it belongs to BARBARA GABLINKSI, his wife, who died almost a full month before him.

Well, at least they'll be beside one another for eternity, he ruminated, his lips pressed tightly together in a sad smile.

He suddenly remembered that he had been standing at about that exact spot a month earlier when he thought he heard a similar faint screaming. He shrugged, figuring he must be hearing things after all, then restarted the engine of the trimmer. He went on his way, exercising great care as he trimmed around the headstones.

Remonstrance
Patricia Gomes

They can't hear
above the din.
Shrieks
of unmasked fear,
weighted guilt,
and bare-faced bewilderment
confound
their long-held beliefs
while torrential tears
of unapologetic grief
pound against
the hard-shelled backs
of muttering beetles.
     Relentless,
          ceaseless.

Every one of them prayed
death
would be quieter.

Beguiled by a Melancholy Knell
Lee Clark Zumpe

How many miles Spencer Carson had traveled he could not guess.

Standing in a boreal forest of mixed evergreen coniferous trees and various deciduous species, he felt the world he had always known gradually slipping away into a matterless void. History, science and religion had no meaning here. Memory and experience amounted to nothing.

He came here by himself, as he had been instructed. Yet, he knew he was not alone.

Soon, they would approach. They would peel themselves from the outlying nothingness to attend to the new arrival. If he concentrated his dwindling powers of observation and scanned the immediate setting, he could see them as clearly as one discerns the margins of a dream: slender shadow entities dwelling just outside the boundaries of the visible world; twisted and misshapen forms moving with unnatural kinesthetic urgency. He had been aware of their presence for some time, detecting one or two contorted beings following him throughout the course of his journey. They acted as insistent escorts, monitoring his progress as he traveled through unfamiliar territory and influencing his every decision.

Here, their numbers were far too great to tally.

In scattered patches beneath jack pine and quaking aspen, the ground hinted at vast stretches of unmarked graves. It signaled to any uninvited wanderer that countless corpses resided in that remote burial place, each enwrapped in its winding sheet and consigned to everlasting, uneasy slumber in a sprawling necropolis.

No uninvited wanderers found their way to those unconsecrated acres, though – of this, Spencer Carson was quite certain, given the fact that to reach his destination he felt as if he had somehow passed through an inexplicable barrier into an alien milieu. No one could find such a place unless they had been beckoned. He could not remember when he first heard their call. He only knew he could no longer resist their summons – and that no one who noticed his absence would come looking for him.

* * *

Once he cleared the Canadian border, Bryce Irwin stayed on the deserted two-lane highway making his way north along a meandering asphalt ribbon that pushed deep into the wilderness of Alberta and British Columbia. His carefully chosen route kept him west of Calgary and Edmonton, skirting the Elk Range of the Canadian Rockies beneath the double summit of Mount Pocaterra. Built by a private enterprise in the 1930s, the motorway had been largely abandoned by its owners near the end of the 20th century. Most travelers opted to drive Highway 93, since few modern maps – be they traditional or digital – identified this road as an option.

No one stopped him at the border crossing. No barrier obstructed his path. An old guard post crouched along the roadway, long abandoned and in disrepair. A sign, pockmarked by buckshot, notified travelers that they were about to enter Canada, but offered no jovial welcome nor promises of hospitality. Bryce slowed momentarily before resuming his race into uncharted territory.

"How long have we been driving?" Safira Amuata, Bryce's common law wife, spoke with grim resignation she did not bother to conceal. Though she had accepted the gravity of the evolving calamity he had revealed to her, her understanding of his strategy left her strangely indifferent to its success. If the world was really ending, she would have preferred to watch its demise on the 55-inch flat screen TV in the comfort of their living room. "How much farther?"

"I don't know, 10 hours since we left home?" Bryce checked the odometer, but the numbers it reported made little sense to him. In the fever dream that had become his reality, measurements of time and distance no longer applied. "I think we've got another 800 miles to go. I'll have to stop and fill up the tank before we get there. There's a little settlement near Utikuma Lake. Should be a place there."

"Do you think they'll have food?"

"We have plenty of provisions in the trunk," Bryce said, almost snapping at her. "No need to risk direct contact."

"Don't call them 'provisions,'" she said. "It sounds so unappetizing. 'Snacks,' or 'munchies' would be more appealing."

"Fine," Bryce said, frustrated by her apparent apathy. "We have plenty of 'snacks' in the trunk."

He now regretted his decision to ask her to accompany him. It had not been part of the plan. The instructions he received made no mention of her. Her presence might cause his gracious hosts to refuse his admittance.

"I'd still like a fresh cup of coffee when we get there." She looked out the window. The forest crowded the slender highway. Weedy undergrowth spilled onto the pavement. Overhead, through occasional breaks in the foliage, the color of the sky seemed wrong. "Maybe a donut or an apple fritter."

"Just remember that we can't waste any time." Bryce recalled the vision he had shared with her a few days earlier. He assured her it was no dream – he had been wide awake when he experienced it. He interpreted it as both prophecy and divine inspiration. The message, though difficult to decipher, had instilled a certain sense of urgency he could not ignore. "We don't have much time. That's what they said: *Don't miss this opportunity. Limited time offer.*"

* * *

Wilfred Pearson stood within a clump of leafy trees set on the gentle slope of a well-maintained lawn outside a rambling office complex in Edmonton. Looking rough and unkempt, he paced to and fro, repeatedly trampling the same blades of grass beneath his wingtips. He held fast to an empty foam cup that previously contained cheap convenience store coffee.

Wilfred glanced at his watch, frowning. He could not fault Tisha Hewitt for her tardiness: He had misread her most recent text message and arrived an hour early. When it came to communication, he preferred phone conversations to emails and private messages. A self-professed anachronism, the private investigator – who actually favored the antiquated term *private eye* – had practically fallen out of a 1970s primetime detective series, driving around town in his vintage Pontiac Firebird and tracking down bail jumpers.

Much to his irritation, most of his workload these days consisted of agency assigned insurance investigations involving worker's compensation claims and personal injury cases. The agency avoided the sleazier jobs, opting to stay out of bad relationships and broken marriages. When Wilfred needed fast cash, he might latch onto one of those gigs, stalking an errant partner hoping to catch evidence of adultery.

He needed some fast cash right now.

That fact brought about the impromptu meeting with Tisha Hewitt in the parking lot of the predominantly abandoned office complex which currently housed the vacant headquarters of businesses that had been shuttered during the pandemic. Aside from a few struggling entrepreneurships that had survived the shutdown, the administrative center had become a sepulcher of failed enterprises. Only a handful of vehicles clustered in one corner of the parking lot confirmed the presence of leaseholders.

Hewitt had offered the private eye a generous sum for information from his private case files. Ostensibly, she wanted to pick his brain about a couple of missing person cold cases he had worked 20-odd years ago. Given the amount of money she had offered him, Wilfred suspected she might want more than just insight and intel.

The woman who made such a charitable offer and arranged this weekday rendezvous once worked as an award-winning investigative reporter for a Chicago daily. She now made a living as a freelance journalist writing for a variety of specialty publications covering subjects ranging from anthropology, archaeology and folklore to esoteric literature and paranormal phenomena.

At the exact time she had indicated in her recent text, Tisha pulled up driving a rental luxury sedan that looked as if it came straight from a dealer's showroom. She stayed in the car, rolled the passenger window down and compared the disheveled middle-aged fellow outside to a 20-year-old headshot of Wilfred posted on the investigative agency's website.

"I guess that's you," she said with the hint of a smile. "May as well get in. We've got a long drive ahead of us."

"I didn't know we were going – "

"Of course, you didn't," Tisha said. "I got a lead and decided to follow it. You can tell me about your cases on the way. I don't know this region very well, so I'd prefer to have someone along who's familiar with the lay of the land."

"I thought you just wanted information," Wilfred said, leaning against the rental car. "I didn't prep for field work."

"Consider yourself a tour guide for now, if that's amenable." Tisha reached over and opened the car door, silently compelling him to take a seat. "I'll make it worth your while. Double my offer for your services. Triple it if we run into trouble – which seems unlikely."

"Fine," Wilfred said, lurching his exhausted frame into the car. The cases the agency had assigned him could wait. He did need the money. "But, you should expect trouble. Trouble always finds me."

* * *

Friesen's Outpost stood on the northeast corner of a remote crossroads surrounded by a vast landscape of muskeg, low hills and distant, ragged lines of seemingly impenetrable forest. The gas pumps had been recently upgraded, with modern steel canopies and sleek outdoor lighting that clashed with the vintage aesthetic of the store. The original building could have been assembled more than a century ago, and despite all attempts to renovate, refashion and rebrand it, the place still felt like an intrusive frontier garrison reluctantly occupying space in inhospitable territory.

Shrouded by a sea of gray clouds, the absence of the sun rendered a surreal netherworld that felt wholly camouflaged to those too oblivious to be cognizant of anything beyond the artificial constructs our limited senses identified.

As Bryce Irwin filled the gas tank, he scanned the bleak and beautiful reaches of the terrain, simultaneously entranced and distressed by its unearthly beauty. He wondered if anyone else who passed by this intersection could comprehend the fantastic, grotesque panorama that now saturated his vision, its breadth filled with preternatural attributes, abhorrent and unnamable hues, and glimpses of monstrous overseers who, ever observant, scrutinize all space and time from their lofty perches.

Bryce mused, almost absent-mindedly, that even these may be figments of his imagination, fabricated out of a necessity to impose order to chaos.

Bryce admitted to himself that Safira Amuata polluted his life with chaos. She worked an endless series of menial temp jobs with no prospect of advancement. She showed no interest in pursuing further education or learning a trade. She had distanced herself from her few living relatives, and remained socially disengaged and estranged from anyone who had ever made overtures of friendship.

For some reason, though, she had latched onto to Bryce.

He met her more than a dozen years earlier at a paranormal convention that featured seminars and panel discussions on ghost hunting, psychic mediumship, UFO theories and demonology. Safira – who dabbled in fortune telling – had given a lecture on astrology and numerology. He caught up with her in the vendor room where she was hawking oracle cards.

After a few pleasant dates, she invited herself to move into his comfortable two-bedroom home in a peaceful suburban neighborhood with easy access to public parks, shopping malls and entertainment venues. He welcomed the prospect of companionship, and felt confident that affection would eventually blossom – and it had, though neither felt comfortable expressing tenderness and devotion.

"I'm getting a cup of coffee," Safira said, diverting him from his ponderings. He shot her a disapproving glance, knowing she would pay him no heed. She examined her reflection in the car window briefly, removing a black-and-white scrunchie from her hair. Instead of tossing it in the backseat to get lost amongst the clutter, she placed the hair tie on her husband's wrist – knowing it would probably annoy him. "Hold onto this for me, babe. Do you want anything?"

"No, thank you." He knew better than to try to stop her. He did not want to make a scene – not here, not this close to his destination. They were watching him. Judging him. Imploring him to do what needed to be done. "Just don't be long," he said, maintaining a calm but assertive tone. "I don't want to keep them waiting."

A bell jingled as Safira walked through the front door of Friesen's Outpost. At 6 p.m., the store had no customers. A clerk balanced on a stool behind a counter just inside the entrance, his eyes glassily staring at the ceiling. He may have acknowledged Safira's presence with a submissive nod, but followed with no verbal greeting.

Despite Bryce's advice, she proceeded at a leisurely pace, unhurriedly sauntering up one aisle and down the next, inspecting the sparsely populated shelves and admiring an inventory of groceries and essentials with unfamiliar brand names and exotic packaging. Bags of potato chips, plastic-wrapped trays of cookies, and cans of nuts dominated one entire fixture, while various sizes of bottled soft drinks subjugated a compact freezer section on the back wall of the establishment. A freestanding refrigerated unit had been stocked with pre-made sandwiches, wraps, and salads. Hot dogs rotated perpetually on silver rollers beneath red-hot heating elements, condemned to that scorching inferno like sinners stuffed into cellulose casings and sent to burn in eternal flames.

Through the window, Safira could see Bryce outside by the gas pump, fingering buttons to indicate that he had completed his transaction and wanted a printed receipt. In a moment, he would reclaim his spot in the driver's seat, ready to take the wheel and plunge even further into this unfamiliar territory. Seized by uncompromising determination, he would continue heading toward an unknown fate, based upon a prophetic vision that hinted at an impending cataclysm.

She poured herself a cup of coffee, wondering if it might be her last.

"So, has it started yet?" As Safira approached the cashier, she noticed a small tablet propped up against an oversized jar of pickled eggs on the counter. Though he had the device muted, she could see enough of the screen to realize he had some 24-hour news livestream playing. "What's happening?"

"Sorry, ma'am?" The clerk had long hair and a scruffy beard. His nametag proclaimed him to be Herman, but offered no other clues as to his position or job performance. "Not sure what you mean."

"You know – the end of the world," she said with a slight laugh, not sure whether she would come across as a concerned citizen or a half-crazed alarmist. "The beginning of the end?"

"No more than usual, I guess," Herman said. He leaned forward, falling off of the stool and onto his feet. He offered her a look that reassured her he did not find the question overtly weird. "I grew up in the '70s and '80s. For my generation, we woke up thinking it might be doomsday."

"Gen Xer, huh?" His easygoing, calming demeanor put her at ease. "Independent. Known for your adaptability. Raised with minimal supervision."

"That pretty much sums it up." Herman started scanning the items Safira had collected in a shopping basket. She assembled an odd assortment of snacks like an animal foraging for survival. "Where are you headed?"

"North," Safira said. "Somewhere. Not sure if the place even has a name."

"You'll know it when you get there," Herman said. As he continued bagging her groceries, she noticed a curious tattoo on his forearm depicting a jackal-headed man. He saw her staring at the image, seemingly mesmerized by it. "You'll know you have arrived when it feels like you belong."

"I like that," Safira said, swiping her credit card and awaiting further instructions. She spent far more than she should have, but given the circumstances, adding to her debt seemed like the least of her worries. "You sound like you might moonlight as a soothsayer." She felt foolish when he ignored her attempt at humor. To recover, she complimented his ink. "That's a cool tattoo Is it Egyptian?"

"Sort of," he said, rewarding her admiring comment with a languid smile. "It combines elements of Egyptian and Graeco-Roman mythology," Herman explained. "It's kind of a hybrid figure." He paused, following his customer's gaze to the car parked by the gas pumps. The man in the driver's seat had his hands on the steering wheel. His eyes, wide, focused on something indistinct and irresistible in the gray distance. "Looks like your friend is waiting for you."

"Boyfriend," Safira said. "Husband, I guess – just never got around to the formality of having a ceremony."

"Maybe there's a reason for that."

"Look," Safira said, closing her eyes. "Is there any chance I could just pop out the backdoor?" She hesitated, surprised at herself for finding the courage to walk away from him after so many years. But he had changed – he had grown detached and despondent. She had tried – many times – to goad him into counseling. He always found a way to avoid it. "I know this sounds terrible, but I don't think I can go where he's going. If he comes looking for me, will you tell him …" Her voice trailed off as she tried to find the right words. "I don't know what to say to him."

"Don't worry, ma'am," Herman said. "I'll take you back to the breakroom and you can wait there until he's gone." The clerk circled the counter and walked over to the front of the store. He took the precaution of locking the door, but he knew it was unnecessary. "He won't come in looking for you. He's too far gone now. He's too close. Their call is too powerful. In a few more minutes, he'll forget about you and just keep going."

"How do you know that?"

"My father – he heard them, too. Had a vision. Packed up all our belongings in a beat-up station wagon that could barely get from one side of town to the other, and drove up here from Florida." Herman stood at the front door, watching Safira's husband as he slowly yielded to his obsession. Whatever connection Bryce still had to his wife slowly ebbed as the compulsion to complete his journey intensified. "My dad abandoned me. Left me with some folks at a little settlement near here. I was 10."

"What about your mother?"

"She died about a year before that," Herman said. "Cancer. Slow and merciless. We watched her slip away, little by little. Nothing we could do to stop it. Nothing we could do to make it painless."

"I'm so sorry," Safira said. "What happened to your father?"

"I don't know for sure," Herman said. "I guess he found whatever it was he was looking for out there – found where he felt like he belonged."

A few minutes later, Bryce Irwin pulled out of the Friesen's Outpost parking lot and headed north on a deserted two-lane highway, heading deeper into the Canadian wilderness.

* * *

Investigative reporter Tisha Hewitt had driven roughly four hours north out of Edmonton by the time Wilfred Pearson, a cantankerous private eye whose clothes reeked of cigarettes and whiskey, notified her that he had failed to follow up on a recent lead that could be connected to one of his decades-old cold cases.

"No one is asking about those two anymore," he said in his defense. "Besides, I can't just make my own rules. The agency prioritizes my workload. Those cases may not be solved, but they aren't going to bring in any revenue either. That's why they aren't important to the agency."

"But they're important to someone." Tisha felt a pang of exasperation, aggravated that her temporary partner could show such apathy. "And if there's a connection between all these disappearances, then finding out what's happening may keep other people from becoming victims."

"I don't know," Wilfred said, sounding skeptical of her theory. "People go missing all the time. Thousands every year, without a trace. No sketchy backgrounds suggesting foul play. No evidence of fraud. No suicide notes. Just gone, like they vanished into thin air."

"I know all that." Tisha surveyed the hilly landscape of central Alberta, with deciduous forest stands clustered along the horizon like ancient gods converging and conspiring to influence the fate of humanity. Mile after mile passed by without a sign of human life. "By your own admission, though, there's a common thread here. Even though we can't drop a pin on the map yet, some of these people seem to be heading for the same destination. That has to mean something."

"Yes," he admitted. "It could." Wilfred grumbled, silently rereading notes he had already gone over a dozen times in the last few days. During the drive, he had shared the highlights of his investigations with Tisha, but now he started to recall details of each case that he had not recorded at the time. "Let me see: The first case – the one from 1997 – was a 37-year-old school teacher from South Carolina. Single, no children. Parents both deceased. Coworkers reported her missing when she didn't report for work after winter holidays."

"Who hired you to find her?"

"An insurance company," he said. "She had a life insurance policy through the teacher's union."

"Who was the beneficiary?"

"Some local animal shelter." He searched for the name. "Last Hope Animal Rescue of Myrtle Beach. In her will, she split up her estate among several charities."

"Doesn't sound like someone who just walks away from her life," Tisha said, trying to construct a mental image of the woman. "Did you find anything that explained why she came to Alberta?"

"No. She had never even traveled outside the United States before that trip." Wilfred remembered visiting some of the places she had been seen before falling off the grid completely: a motor lodge outside Great Falls, Montana; a rest stop in the border town of Coutts on I-15; a diner in Leduc, Alberta. One witness he spoke to put her on the campus of Athabasca University about a week after she is thought to have left her studio apartment in Conway, South Carolina. "A couple of people I spoke to said she seemed preoccupied – unfocused. Like she was walking around in a dream."

"That's interesting," Tisha said. "The guy I'm trying to track down was the same way before he disappeared, according to his closest friends." A wealthy Massachusetts family had hired Tisha to write a story about its missing patriarch, Spencer Carson. Prior to his disappearance, Carson helmed Armitage Capital Management, a Boston-based private investment firm. "One of them even thought he may have had some kind of early-onset dementia."

"The teacher used her credit card at a gas station near Utikuma Lake," Wilfred said. "We're not far from there now, actually."

"What about the other case?"

"Around the same area," Wilfred said. He flipped through more pages of hastily scribbled notes searching for a specific name. "So, this guy was on his honeymoon in Niagara Falls. He gets into a fight with his wife, leaves her on their wedding night, and she never sees him again."

"Charming," Tisha said. "Seems like she may have dodged a bullet."

"Well, the local law enforcement officials tried to pin it on her, but couldn't make it stick," Wilfred said. "They had it in their heads that she pushed him into the river – he goes over the falls, and his body is never recovered."

"Seems risky," Tisha said. "No way to guarantee that he wouldn't wash ashore downstream."

"Exactly." Wilfred glanced up at the scenery, realizing they were approaching a small, remote community. "This was in 2010, and it was a little easier to track his movements. He spent more than half a week traveling from New York through Ohio, Indiana, Illinois, Wisconsin, Minnesota and North Dakota before he finally crossed the border into Saskatchewan. He took his time, favoring backroads over the Interstate system and staying at out-of-the-way motels along the way. Plenty of people remembered seeing him – none of them had much to say about him."

"Where did the trail go cold?"

"Between Saskatoon and Edmonton," he said. "At least, until a few months ago."

"That's when you got the call?" Tisha started mentally organizing the details of Wilfred's two cold cases. After hours of assessing his rambling dialog, she felt like she had garnered the pertinent minutiae and could begin to make connections beyond the obvious. She encouraged him to continue, grateful he had finally circled back to the recent lead he had ignored. "You said someone contacted you with new information."

"More like a confession," Wilfred said. "Although, it's second-hand, so you have to take that into consideration." He paused, closing his notebook and stuffing it back into an oversized envelope for legal documents. "I don't have it on paper," he admitted, and for a moment, he sensed Tisha's rising displeasure. Before she had a chance to criticize him, he pulled out his phone. "I still have the voicemail message."

"Mr. Pearson, I've been trying to reach you," the voice stated, sounding troubled but unwavering. I understand you tried to find a man named Leon Hodge many years ago. I think he's my father. My mother, who died recently, told me what happened. She said she only spoke to him once after he left her, and that he wouldn't come back even when she told him she was pregnant. She told me he called her from a payphone in Canada, at a store called Friesen's Outpost. If you have any more information, I would appreciate it if you could contact me."

As the recording finished, Tisha's rental sedan reached a remote crossroads surrounded by a vast landscape of muskeg, low hills and distant, ragged lines of seemingly impenetrable forest. On the northeast corner of the intersection sat a gas station with modern pumps and an adjoining convenience store that looked like it dated back more than a century.

Just as a heavy bank of clouds crawled across the sky effectively obscuring the noonday sun, Tisha and her dumbfounded passenger pulled into the parking lot of Friesen's Outpost.

* * *

Sometime between midnight and dawn, Bryce Irwin abandoned his car. Its usefulness had ceased – much like his own sense of value had slowly declined in recent years. Exactly when his tires left the pavement he did not recall. The road had long since disappeared, swallowed by the night's impermeable darkness and the region's vast boreal forests punctuated by bogs and wetlands. It seemed to him miraculous that he had managed to infiltrate this wilderness at all, given the circumstances.

It seemed extraordinary that he had made it as far as he had.

Now on foot, he shambled along with bowed head, his thoughts nothing more than dwindling artifacts of disappearing knowledge. Wisdom had been superseded by a jumble of impulses introduced by external forces. Sedimentary layers of memory eroded as the peace and serenity of solitude, vacuity, and eternal silence came flooding over his mind. Irresistible, disembodied voices supplanted all reason and common sense. He wandered without any objective in mind other than *their* objective, lacking any sense of purpose other than *their* purpose.

And at some point in his arduous trek, as his feet trudged across the dewy ground, he realized how long it had been since he had first heard their haunting knell. Some part of him felt awe – and a certain sense of pride – that he had managed to resist them for so many years. No one realized how long he had heard their whispered calls.

But he was so tired now. How could anyone blame him for capitulating to those ever-present solicitations inviting him to recede into the promise of idyllic nothingness?

As the twin beams of his car's headlights faded into the distance behind Bryce, he glanced skyward as if the stars innumerable might afford some final vestige of clarity, but he found only more evidence of his own irrelevance: He felt meager and meaningless beneath the incomprehensible vastness of the awful, infinite universe. He felt eager to divest himself of his lingering identity – to lose himself among the constellations in the boundless cosmos.

Those stars overhead were not his stars. The ground beneath his feet was no longer that of any terrestrial domain. Bryce had stumbled completely off the map, into some uncharted region, surrounded by vast stretches of unmarked graves in a secret, sprawling necropolis. All along the darkened path he followed, he sensed the tombs in which forgotten dead lay quietly enshrined, all deprived of funerary ritual: No bells tolled to draw the grief-stricken, and no mourners came to wail and weep.

He soon found himself standing on the bank of a broad, torpid river whose mesmeric murmur echoed the melancholic mood of this surreal netherworld. Surveying the waterway's slow, serpentine course, he now detected a throng of slender shadow entities gathering like carrion crows circling a sick cow in its pasture. He watched them as they moved with unnatural kinesthetic necessity, no longer able to conceal their exhilaration nor their insatiability.

They had taken advantage of Bryce's insecurity and anxiety. They had cultivated his hopelessness, making him believe he was insignificant. They had ensnared him, and now these twisted and misshapen wraiths waited for him to take the last few steps into the river, cutting himself off from everything he ever knew. His final act of acquiescence would bring him wholly into their sphere.

Bryce stood there, searching his fading memory for something meaningful. They flitted from one patch of gloom to the next, flocking in ever greater numbers like moving masses of ghastliness eager to pounce upon the frailty of their prey. They pushed against the very boundaries of reality, squirming like ravenous grave worms. He felt them crowding in behind him, still locked in their incorporeal forms, goading and prodding and provoking him.

Threatened by their proximity, he raised his arms to hinder their cold embrace. It was at that moment he saw his wife's black-and-white scrunchie, still wrapped around his wrist.

* * *

Tisha Hewitt had no difficulty finding an open space at the gas pumps.

At first glance, passersby traveling Highway 88 might believe Friesen's Outpost had gone out of business. The only conspicuous evidence that the place was still operational came in the form of LCD advertising displays mounted on the pumps and the uncanny glow of fluorescent lights spilling through the front window of the store. A young woman, looking bedraggled and exhausted, sat with her legs tucked beneath her on a weathered bench outside the business.

"Would you mind filling up the tank?" Tisha smiled at her passenger as she reached into the backseat and retrieved her purse. "I'll go inside, pick up something to drink, ask a few questions. Maybe whoever's in there will have some information."

"About a 14-year-old cold case?" Wilfred Pearson grimaced as he unbuckled his seatbelt. "Seems pretty unlikely."

"My case is a little more recent," Tisha reminded him. "I've got loads of photos. Maybe they'll remember seeing my guy – especially if I tell them about the reward."

"Reward?" The word brought an inappropriate smile to Wilfred's lips. "I'm starting to think maybe I saw your guy."

Although they had only driven four hours north out of Edmonton, the climate was noticeably different. The air had a chilly touch for this time of year, and its keen edge made Wilfred shudder when he first noticed it. Standing outside Friesen's Outpost, he became aware of a growing sense of unaccountable trepidation. He felt strangely uncomfortable, as if he had unknowingly provoked some unseen force that now calculated his demise. He felt as though he had blundered into a hornet's nest, and retaliation would be quick in coming. The private eye tried to dismiss his uneasiness, telling himself that he had been in far more hazardous situations over the years. Still, the stubborn anxiety lingered.

Their uneventful drive into Alberta's sprawling wilderness left him oddly untethered and vulnerable.

Going over the old cases had dredged up thoughts and impulses he believed he had long ago abandoned on the floor of his psychologist's office. Though he hated to admit it, those mandatory therapy sessions – required by his bosses at the agency after a standard evaluation exposed a parade of red flags – had been undoubtedly benefitted him.

It had been many years since intrusive thoughts had bubbled up to the surface to distract him.

Inside, Tisha questioned a long-haired store clerk named Herman about the disappearance of Armitage Capital Management CEO Spencer Carson. She explained that the man had gone missing 10 months earlier, and several anonymous sources placed him in the vicinity of Utikuma Lake, possibly in Atikameg.

"It's a big area to cover." The clerk tilted his head to one side and ran his fingers through his beard, feigning interest. "I don't remember the name."

"How about the face?" Tisha pulled out her phone and scrolled through half a dozen photos of Carson. "Does he look familiar at all?"

"Can't say that he does, ma'am." Herman shrugged and scanned the two bottles of water she had placed on the counter. "Is that all?"

The former investigative journalist scrutinized the setting. When she first entered the store, the clerk – a tall, slender man well into his 50s wearing jeans and a uniform shirt – had been perched on a stool, his nose buried in some salacious magazine with a lurid cover. Clearly not expecting a lunchtime rush of customers, he awkwardly stashed the publication on a nearby table, hoping it went unnoticed. Tisha could see Herman's copy of the newest issue of *Wicked Worship*, but made no mention of it. She did not recognize the publication.

"Gas," Tisha said, looking back over her shoulder to see if Wilfred had finished. Although the car was still where she parked it, there was no sign of the private investigator she had hired for the day. For a moment, his unexpected absence startled her, and she felt a wave of inexplicable dread. She shook off the sudden urge to run outside and call his name, fearful that he had somehow fallen victim to the plague of unexplained disappearances. She told herself he had probably wandered off to use the restrooms at the rear of the building. "We're on pump 4."

"Great." Herman instinctively followed her gaze outside, and his eyes betrayed a nervousness Tisha had not detected previously. Something out there caused him to waver, if only for an instant. In that instant, she saw through his façade: He was hiding something. His subsequent question confirmed her suspicions, revealing his sudden interest in their immediate plans. "Where are you headed, ma'am?"

"I guess we'll probably head back to Edmonton," Tisha told him, lying. "Unless there's anyone else around here you can think of who might have information about Mr. Carson."

"I'm sorry," Herman said. Having completed the transaction, he stepped back from the counter. "I wish I could be of assistance, ma'am. People around here don't talk much to strangers. I just don't think they'd be much help to you."

"Well, if you happen to think of anything, I'll leave you my contact information." Tisha pulled a business card out of her wallet and placed it on the counter. As Herman reached for it, she noticed the tattoo on his forearm depicting a jackal-headed man. "That's quite elaborate," she said, admiring it before he pulled his arm behind his back. "I don't think I've ever seen such a detailed portrayal of Hermanubis." She considered asking the clerk if he would mind if she snapped a picture of the tattoo, but the panic in his eyes convinced her to resist the urge. "Now, correct me if I'm wrong: Doesn't he conduct the souls of the dead to the underworld?"

"I wouldn't know, ma'am." Herman hesitated, trying to fabricate a believable lie. "Got it a long time ago in college. One of those things you do when you're young and stupid and drunk."

"Yeah," Tisha said, smiling. "Well, at least it's interesting," she added. "You could have ended up with something embarrassing."

As she turned to leave, she was relieved to see that Wilfred was back inside the rental car.

By the time Tisha Hewitt had walked from the front door of Friesen's Outpost to the luxury sedan, she had concluded that Herman not only recognized Spencer Carson but knew exactly what had happened to him. She did not need to dig any further for the moment: Any confrontational questioning might compromise the subsequent criminal investigation. She had plenty of connections in the law enforcement community – even in Alberta. She would follow the proper procedures and notify the authorities. She could then work the story from the sidelines, letting officials solve the case.

"I've got everything I need for now," Tisha said. "Maybe we should call it a day and head back to Edmonton."

"We can't," Wilfred said. He nudged toward the backseat. "We picked up a passenger."

Someone moved underneath a quilt that had not been there earlier. Safira Amuata peeled the cover down just below her eyes. In her gaze Tisha saw desperation.

"Please," Safira said. "I don't feel safe here. I'll explain everything. Just head north."

* * *

"How is this possible?" Former investigative journalist Tisha Hewitt found herself hiking across rolling grassland interspersed with groves of aspen. Saskatoon serviceberry, choke cherry, snow berry and other shrubs provided groundcover. They all paid close attention to their surroundings, knowing this territory to be hunting grounds for wolves, grizzly bears, black bears, and cougars. "How can this be here without anyone knowing about it?"

Following the instructions of Safira Amuata, Tisha had driven north on a well-maintained highway, passing by turnoffs for Red Earth Creek and Loon Lake and Little Buffalo. After crossing the Wabasca River, they continued for some time before turning onto an unmarked, unpaved path that pushed deep into the boreal forest. As they drove, Safira recounted her own tragic tale along with her shame.

"I shouldn't have let him go," she kept saying, full of regret. "I shouldn't have let him come up here at all."

Bryce Irwin – Safira's common law husband – had apparently found his way to this place. Persuaded by voices of things he thought were prophets, he had begged her to accompany him, promising her that it was their only chance at surviving some coming apocalypse. As he drew closer to his destination, she grew more wary of the situation. She knew he had struggled with depression, but all her attempts to encourage him to seek professional help had failed.

"I couldn't go with him," she told them. "I didn't know what to do."

Bryce had deserted her two days ago, leaving her Friesen's Outpost. He drove away as though he had forgotten she existed.

Although her story sounded unbelievable, the scene before them now lent it undeniable truth and plausibility.

For as far they could see, hundreds of abandoned cars and trucks littered the landscape. The vehicles had been left to rot in the eerily tranquil meadow, slowly disintegrating as vegetation and the elements encroached. Some had already fragmented into unrecognizable bits, forsaken by former owners whose fates likely remained a mystery. Some had partially collapsed, transforming into rusty skeletons that radiated despair and neglect. A few remained practically intact, not yet ready to disperse into the ecosystem.

"There are hundreds of them." Wilfred Pearson promenaded from one car to the next, overwhelmed by the grim tableau. "Some of these go back decades – 50 years or more."

"Herman told me it's been happening for centuries," Safira said. "He said it affected the people who lived here before the settlers arrived."

"I knew he was hiding something," Tisha said. "How does he know about this?"

"He said his father abandoned him when he was a kid," Safira explained. "The people who took him in and raised him are like caretakers of this place. They come up here regularly to collect the bodies and bury them." She searched the landscape, hoping to find their car. "He told me how to find this place," she said. "I think he wanted to bring me here. I don't know what he was going to do, but he didn't want me leave."

"Jesus." Wilfred muttered under his breath. He wondered how many cold case files could be solved just by snapping photos of the license plates scattered across the somber landscape. As he continued his tour of the terrain, he felt pangs of anguish and waves of rage. More than Tisha Hewitt ever could, he empathized with poor Bryce Irwin. He understood the inclination to surrender to despair. He recognized the voices that coaxed him even now. "We can't stay here," he said, stopping in his tracks. "It will be getting dark soon."

In the distance, Wilfred saw the menacing edge of a boreal forest. It felt strangely out of synch with the surrounding countryside, as if it existed in between two distinct realities. Even the ground upon which they currently stood seemed somehow contrived, a preternatural fabrication visible only to those who had been inadvertently drawn into an uncanny entanglement.

"You're right." Tisha recognized it now, too. She sensed an imminent ambush as her gaze locked on the setting sun. With only another hour of daylight at most, she knew they needed to backtrack and regroup. "We'll come back as soon as I can explain all this to the authorities." She quickly took a series of photographs with her phone, knowing the pictures would provide ample proof to launch an exhaustive investigation. "Safira, get back into the – "

Tisha saw something in the distance, approaching them. Tall and slender, it shambled stiffly, its head bowed and its arms gripping its abdomen. It seemed oblivious to its surroundings. Behind it, a throng of twisted and misshapen wraiths mustered at the edge of the forest, crowding into shadows beneath the jack pine and quaking aspen. The distance and the darkness conspired to mask any distinguishable features these entities might have possessed, but Tisha knew instinctively that they were not of this world.

"I told you," Wilfred said as the solitary figure approached them, its gait erratic as it quickened its pace. "Trouble always finds me."

"Get in," Tisha shouted, her foot hovering above the accelerator. "We've got to get out of here."

The thing raised one of its arms into the air, waving pitifully.

"Wait," Safira said. Even at this distance, she could see it: It was Bryce, and he still had her scrunchie wrapped around his wrist. "It's him!"

* * *

"Nothing?" Wilfred Pearson sat across a small table in a trendy café in downtown Edmonton. "Nothing at all?"

"Not a thing," Tisha Hewitt said, sipping on coffee. "We tried at least a dozen little paths splitting off from Highway 88. Honestly, every one of them looked the same. Every one of them led nowhere."

"But you showed them the photos?"

"I showed them." She pulled out her phone and started flipping through the pictures she had taken of the abandoned cars. Every image showed nothing but empty landscape. "It's like we imagined the entire thing. Mass hallucination. Except, you know, it wasn't."

"There has to be a way to find it again," Wilfred said. The voices he had heard that day had gradually subsided. He did not want to invite them back into his head. "Satellite images? Aerial reconnaissance?"

"They've already done all that." Tisha had experienced similar phenomena in the past. Some things did not want to be uncovered. Some things needed to remain hidden for the benefit of humanity. "Even Friesen's Outpost is shuttered," she added. "Law enforcement did manage to track down the guy that worked there – Herman Hurlbut. Had some outstanding warrants. Interpol was also looking for him, too."

"That's something, at least."

"Not really," Tisha said. "A couple of days after they picked him up, he disappeared from his cell in Edmonton Institution. Security cameras show nothing. He just vanished."

"I guess all my cold cases are going back into the freezer," Wilfred said. "It bothers me, though. All of it. They're out there, somewhere, and we were close to finding them. I don't like that they're forgotten, interred by strangers. Their only memorial is a graveyard of rotting cars – and we can't even find that on a map."

"I know," Tisha admitted. She had her story, though the people who funded it might not approve of her findings. She had gleaned some interesting information from her interview with Bryce Irwin – things that she hesitated to put in print. She believed him at his word, but she wondered what others might make of his brush with the unknown. "It's going to be hard to let them go."

"My therapist told me something once," Wilfred said. "She said 'it's not about letting them go. It's about letting go of the feeling you failed them." The private eye offered a somber smile and wagged his head. "We did everything we could do. Sometimes, there's nothing that can take away the emptiness. You just channel your energy into something that gives you structure and purpose – even if that something is temporary and mundane."

"Indeed," Tisha agreed. "Something is almost always preferable to nothingness."

Mourning the Nameless Ones
by Amanda Bergloff

The Call Stop
Kendra Preston Leonard

It was a beautiful early autumn. The Long War of 1914-1927 was almost fifty years in the past, and I'd come to a small town an hour or so east of London to study the history of the town's famous Shakespeare festival, the only one that had kept going through the entire conflict, all thirteen years of it. I had rented rooms in the outskirts of the town, and the windows that ran along the entire side of my bedroom and writing area looked out onto a field of yellow flowers, swaying and shining under the fall-tilted light. These were the kind of days that made you want to put work aside in search of a bicycle and a path into the woods, or a long stroll along a creek.

My lodgings had been converted out of old train cars: the rectangular windows with their sliding mechanisms and rounded corners, the tiny, odd hallways between rooms, and the long, narrow rooms themselves all told the story of a collection of cars patched together and modernized into a quaint collection of suites. I wasn't alone staying there. A man in his twenties named Edward Murthy lived in Flat 1, and Flat 3 was home to Major Fuller, whose full name I never did get. I don't even know where he had served, only that he had come from this village, married a French woman who had died about ten years before, and returned to the village, passing his retirement quietly in it, working crosswords and reading in the shared lounge. While I was working, especially in the long, warm evenings, I often heard the rushing of the new train on its way to or from London, and I also heard the slower rhythms of an older train pulling along local tracks somewhere very close nearby.

On one of these lovely sunny days I realized just how close my rooms were to the old tracks. It was a day I'd planned to spend taking notes of old files from the festival, but the weather had made me restless, and as I heard the train come by and slow, I opened the door in the tiny hallway between my bedroom and sitting room, and the train was right there. Right there, on my doorstep. And it had stopped. Perhaps because I'd opened the door, and the conductor took that as a signal. There was no more than a distance of a foot between my doorway and the door to the carriage, and the train was perfectly even with the door itself. The sun was out and a light breeze was passing through the young trees on the other side of the train and I impulsively stepped into the carriage, and the train began to move.

At the end of the carriage was a group of schoolgirls in the uniforms of the nearby girls' academy. They spread out over several seats, and one girl held a pink leash that was attached to a pink collar on a beautiful and sleek grey dog, who was rolling on her back and offering up her soft belly for petting. "Oh," I said. "What a pretty dog! May I say hello?"

"Of course," said the girl. "This is Theia." I bent to pet the dog, who licked my hands and let me rub her ears.

"I must be missing my dog at home," I said, realizing that I was wearing just a light-yellow housedress made out of a cotton voile and tennis shoes and must have looked like some kind of disorderly, half-dressed person. I felt conspicuously American as well among all of these uniformed girls. I introduced myself and mentioned that I was visiting and researching the festival.

"I'm Myra," said the girl with the dog. The other girls followed in turn, and as the train continued on its slow, curving path, we passed an arts and crafts mansion with a garden full of irises and a deep creek that bounded its front lawn. "You're lucky to get to keep your dog at school," I said. Myra laughed. "Well, no one knows, really. Theia stays with Old Harald, the groundskeeper, and I visit her. She was a present from my mother, so I could hardly give her up, you see? Besides, she loves roaming around in the woods and the school grounds."

The girls talked. Margery, a tall brunette, stretched out along a seat. "I've got a position at a garage for when I'm done here," she said. Helen waved her away. "You can't get anything without college," she said. She looked at me, as if for confirmation from someone older. "Well, college isn't for everyone," I said. "If Margery wants to be a mechanic, she should do it." We were passing an old Italianate villa, decrepit and missing window glass and inner floors. "I like your hat," I told Susan. It was a fancy feathery thing, pinned on above her black curls. "Oh!" she said. "Thanks for the reminder. I have to swap it out before we get to the academy." The other girls wore beret-style hats that went with their sweaters and the grosgrain ribbons that circled the hems of their dark blue skirts. "Does anyone else have a fitting tomorrow?" asked Julie. Three did. A fitting for what, I wondered. "Oh," Julie said. "Our gowns. You get a white academy gown when you enter, and then you get it refitted for the holiday presentations—the big event before you go home for Christmas—and then, for the senior girls, fitted again when you get your diploma in the spring. Then you never have to wear it again!"

"Some do, though," said Lizzie, idly twirling her hair. "Some girls wear them as their wedding dresses."

"They must be very elegant," I said, trying to imagine a dress that could work as both a graduation gown, debutante presentation dress, and wedding dress.

"They have tons of embroidery, white on white, all very virginal," said Helen in a way that suggested she didn't think much of virginity.

"And some never leave the school," added Julie breezily.

Anne jumped in. "That's right. If a girl dies while at school, they put a black band on the gown's sleeve and hang it in the chapel for six months."

"How morbid."

"Yes, well, it doesn't happen often. There was a girl, what a few years ago, Elspeth someone—"

"Coates."

"Yes, Elspeth Coates. She was a trainee nurse in the military and was working over the summer holiday—"

The train began to slow. "I think I'd better get off," I said. "I just hopped on without thinking, and I haven't got a ticket."

"You'd be fine," said Margery. "They don't check for passes until the last stop at the academy, anyway."

I hesitated. "Still—"

"This is a regular station we're coming to," said Lizzie. "You can just cross under the tracks and take the next train that goes back the other way. When you get near your stop, you'll have to press this button to make the train stop, because yours isn't a regular stop; it's a call stop."

I went under the tracks and up to the other side wondering if my door had triggered a call button for the train. I'd have to be careful about that. There were several doors in and out of my flat: there was one at the front of my bedroom, reached by steps under a little porch. That was how I entered the flat. Then there was one at the end of the bedroom (which I was beginning to think of as the bedroom carriage) that led into the tiny hallway. Straight ahead in the tiny hallway—what was ever more clearly an enclosed passage between carriages—was a door to the sitting room. To the right was the door that had opened onto the train platform and must be a call signal. To the right was a door that led to the shared lounge for the flats' residents. A train in the direction of the town came along and duly stopped. I was alone on this one, or at least in my carriage. As we came up to my flat, I pressed a doorbell-like button to signal a stop, but nothing happened. I pressed again, but the train still didn't slow. In exasperation, I reached back behind my seat to a different button, which lit up green when I pressed it. By this time we'd gone past the flats and were headed into town. A man in a conductor's uniform appeared at the door at the front end of the carriage and shouted down to me, "You've got to make sure the button lights up—some of them aren't working. This economy, you know." He turned and walked back into the forward carriage, and the train slowed and came to a stop not too far along, apparently just for me. How lovely to be in a small town where the train will stop for you, I thought. I climbed down and saw that the flats were an easy walk away, and I headed back home, my shoes crunching on the gravel by the rails.

That autumn, on sunny days, I often thought about hopping back on the train to try to catch the girls on their way home again from London to the academy to chat and pet Theia, but I had only a limited time to complete my research, and there were stacks of documents to work through. In the evenings, though, I sometimes took a break and joined Edward and the Major and sometimes Mrs. Featherstone, the landlady, who lived in what used to be a stationmaster's house not nearby, for sherry and talk in the lounge. This Wednesday had been cold and rainy, and the glow of the little electric fire in the lounge and human company was appealing. The Major was in his usual red velvet armchair, sipping his sherry. Edward was sitting on the sofa and Mrs. Featherstone was knitting at the table, a long swath of fabric spread out in front of her. At some point, I noticed that the red armchair had the same fabric on it as the long bench—repurposed from a train bench, no doubt—in my sitting room, and I made a remark about it. "Sitting room?" said Mrs. Featherstone, as though she hadn't quite heard me. "Yes, I said, it's on that long bench that runs along the left-hand side of the room." I hadn't used the sitting room in a long while, and in fact it seemed a mix of sitting room and storage area, as there was a large wardrobe squeezed into it and a few boxes I'd simply stacked up when I'd first taken up residence. Mrs. Featherstone looked worried then for a moment, so I said, "Don't worry, I haven't changed or moved anything there, just put a few boxes to one side. It's nice to read in when I haven't got to take notes."

This thinking about the sitting room was probably what prompted me to go in there the next day, and after I'd been reading a while Mrs. Featherstone came in. "I didn't know you were here," she said, apologizing. "I. Well, I didn't really intend this to be a sitting room for you; it's not been re-done, and there's a lot of old stuff in here." I felt foolish: the door had been open when she'd first shown me the flat, and I assumed that it was mine to use. I stood up right away and apologized and made motions to leave, but she smiled. "it's my fault, and it's fine it you want to keep using the room." She gestured around her. "I just need to clean it out a bit." She opened the wardrobe and inside were sheets, or draperies, or. "Are those academy gowns?" I asked.

"Oh yes," she said. "These are quite old, from the Long War, probably." She pulled one out. It was just like a wedding dress and commencement gown all together, covered in tiny embroideries and seed pearls. "Let's see," she said, pulling up the draped neckline to search inside. "S. E. Davies, 1926. A Welsh girl, it seems. Wonder what happened to her."

"Why would her gown be here?"

"Oh, any reason. Maybe she left before commencement, maybe she wasn't happy at school and didn't want the gown, maybe it was lost, who knows? The previous owner of these flats had been related to someone at the school, I think."

"Wouldn't there be records?" Having met some of the girls, I had been thinking of actually visiting the school and seeing it, perhaps going to a Christmas concert or other public event.

"I suppose they're somewhere out there." Mrs. Featherstone flapped her hand to suggest the outside world and smiled at me. "Your next project, maybe?" She pulled the dress further out of the wardrobe. "Oh," she said. A small black banner drifted down the length of the gown, and we could both see small, careful stitches where it had been sewn to the dress's arm. "Well, that might explain it," I said.

"Yes." Mrs. Featherstone sighed. "There were a number of students and old girls lost in the Long War."

"I was wondering about visiting the school," I said. "Maybe when I take a day off..." Mrs. Featherstone was looking and me oddly.

"The rules about visiting are very strict," she said, emphasizing the "very." "But I could ask around and look into it for you, if you really want to." I didn't understand the sudden severity of her voice. Perhaps one of her grandparents had gone there and died in the war? Perhaps she didn't approve of an old fashioned all-girls' school, or the many rich girls who no doubt attended?

"Please," I said anyway, hoping the stereotype of the brash American would excuse me for pushing. "That would be great."

That weekend I decided to take the train again, just as far as I had the first time, to see the girls. My professional curiosity was starting to take hold; perhaps there were links between the town's famous Shakespeare festival and the school. Maybe some of the girls had trained as actresses because of the festival, or had appeared in it. Myra and Theia were on the train again, with the pretty grey dog now sporting a new purple collar and matching leash. Lizzie was there as well, and a few girls I hadn't met before—Mary, Alice, and a Scottish girl the others called Kirky, because, Mary explained, she belonged to the Church—or Kirk—of Scotland. The weather was gloomy and wet; dark leaves swirled in the stream in front of the arts and crafts house and the irises around the creek's edges had been beaten down into dead stems, flat against the ground. I told the girls that my landlady was storing old academy gowns among her things, but at first they weren't interested, talking quietly about exams and a flu-like illness running around the school. One girl had been sent to the hospital in London for it. But Myra turned the conversation around to the academy things my landlady had. "How odd," she said. "Most of us so love the place, we'd never get rid of anything, much less a white."

I offered up Mrs. Featherstone's suggestions of an unhappy student or one who had left before commencement. I'd forgotten all about the arm band, and then suddenly remembered it as we passed by the ruined villa, its walls stained with the rain. "I forgot," I said, and explained. The girls all turned to Mary, who bit her lip. There was a long pause, and we passed a field, the long grasses of summer now breaking into the mud. "Fine," she said. She turned to me. "My auntie worked at the academy for a long time, that's probably how I got in, and I know a lot about it..." She glared at the other girls. "And I know what you're getting at: yes, there is a black burial dress for if you die while you're a student. And after the white hangs in chapel, it's burnt and the ashes are added to the grave. Now can we change the subject? There's too much death all around—" Then Myra let Theia up onto the train seat and the dog settled across the girls' laps. I asked about visiting the school, and Lizzie explained that if I wrote a letter, I should be able to make an appointment for a tour. The woods began to close in, in their perfectly manicured way, and the train slowed.

"When you visit, bring the dress!" said Myra. "It should probably be returned to the school anyway." I promised I would as I stepped off the train.

Mrs. Featherstone found me a few days later. I was working in my bedroom, which had a long wooden table along one side of the carriage that was perfect for setting out papers and typing up notes on the portable typewriter I'd finally bought in town the week before, when I'd become anxious that I wouldn't be able to get all of the notes I needed by slowly handwriting them.

"The school grounds are still quarantined," she said. Oh, I thought, the flu must have gotten really bad. "But," she said. "There's talk of it finally lifting in December, and I'll see what I can do then."

I celebrated an American-style Thanksgiving in London with friends of my parents, where I told them about my Shakespeare festival research and the strange flats made out of railway cars. "Interesting little place," said Bradley. "You'll have to see more of it before you go home. There's a lovely war memorial in the old boys' school cemetery, and of course there's the historic mayor's home which I think you can tour and a little dressmaking museum—"

"What?" I asked. "The boys' school has its own cemetery?" This sounded rather horrible.

Bradley cleaned his classes with his napkin. "Oh yes, well, the school was there forever, or it seemed like it. Good old military training, so many of the old boys went into the service. The school itself is mostly gone, now, I think the land has been sold for houses and the like, but the cemetery is still there. The girls' school cemetery—"

"The girls have one, too?" I was beginning to wonder what gothic novel I'd stumbled into.

"—much smaller, of course, and closed these days—"

I'd never heard of schools having cemeteries before, but Mrs. Featherstone told me when I returned to the village that the boys' cemetery had actually been expanded into the town cemetery, and that the mayor's house was indeed something to see, with its painted ceilings and art collection.

The next weekend I took the special call train twice. On Saturday I got on around four o'clock, and was alone; either the girls were still under quarantine or were simply too busy for excursions. Back at home, my own students would have been preparing for exams as well. On Sunday, though, I decided to try once more to catch the girls on their way home, and was lucky enough to end up on a train with Lizzie, Mary, Alice, Myra, and of course Theia heading to the academy at around two in the afternoon. They told me that the quarantine had been lifted and everyone was well, and that instead of sending a letter for a tour I should simply plan to come out for the public Christmas concert and they would show me all around. The academy would be putting up posters to advertise the event in the next few weeks.

"You'll love the library," said Myra. "It's got loads of old Shakespeare books and the reading room has stained glass windows showing scenes from the plays."

We were almost at the Italian villa, which now appeared to droop more than ever under the weight of the dark late fall skies. "The dress," I said. "I forgot the dress." They all looked disappointed. "But—why don't we get off before the woods and you can come back with me to see it. It's early enough in the day, isn't it?"

They looked around at one another, starting to smile. "Yes!" said Myra, bouncing in her seat. Theia gave her usual wide grin, tongue hanging out to the side.

"I don't know," said Alice. "Won't the conductor know we're out of school bounds?"

"Come on," Lizzie said. "He never tells anyway. Helen goes to and fro all the time."

Under and up, and onto the next train, and Mary got the button for the call stop. I opened the door to my flat slowly and quietly. I didn't think Mrs. Featherstone would care about my visitors, but I didn't want to get them in trouble, either. "Through here," I said. "This is the sitting room—"

They all gathered around the wardrobe, and I pulled out one dress, and then another. They were identical, save that one had had the armband on it and the other not.

"Just like ours!" said Mary. "They haven't changed at all."

"Mrs. Deering's got the best dressmakers anywhere," said Myra.

Alice handed a dress to Lizzie. Lizzie poked inside, pulling out the tag. She looked up in alarm. "This dress—is this a joke?" She looked at me. "Janet, what is this?"

"What?" I pulled the dress away, but she wouldn't let go.

"Here," she pointed, clutching the dress. "This tag—this is *my name*." The tag read "S. E. Davies, 1926."

"Liz, this tag doesn't say your name—"

"My name is Seren Elizabeth Davies," she said. She was shaking.

"Liz, I'm sure there's been another Davies at your school, it's just coincidence—"

"*1926*," she said, becoming more violent in her shaking. Her eyes were enormous.

"But that's ages—"

"Janet, I think we'd better take Lizzie home," said Myra. The other girls clustered around Lizzie.

"I'm so sorry," I said. "I didn't know—I didn't mean to upset anyone—"

Somehow the train was there the instant they opened the door, and they were gone.

My anxiety about finishing my research led me to complete it all early, and I had several days to see the town in mid-December. I visited the mayor's house and it was, truly, a feast for the eyes. On the way to a local restaurant afterwards, I passed by the museum Bradley had mentioned in London. "Deering's Dressmaking Museum," said a sign at the door. Deering was familiar, and I went inside. It was tiny as far as museums go: there was an exhibition on the main floor about Deering's history as a fabric importer, and then one on the second floor about its famous embroiderers, who had made detailed gowns for princesses and queens and wealthy and important women. In a corner on the second floor was a "white"—an academy dress—on a dressmaker's form. It glowed in the late morning light: the draped silk neckline, the intricate white-on-white stitching, the heavy, open sleeves coming to long points at the wrists, the many folds of the train-like back. I admired it for a few minutes.

"Lovely, isn't it?" said the docent, who had come up the stairs behind me.

"So, does Deering's exist at all now?" I asked. "Who makes the gowns now?"

She smiled gently. "You're American, aren't you? Deering's is gone now, of course, except what you see here, and maybe in the closets of some great ladies. There's no call for the gowns now, you know. So sad."

I was confused. Had the flu come back? Had the school closed in the last two weeks? I'd heard nothing. Or did she simply mean that gowns now were reused? The multiple fittings would make sense then, and that might be the tradition. But another thought tugged at me.

I skipped lunch.

I walked back to the flat, looking carefully at the surroundings. Newly paved streets and sidewalks led to my front door. I went in and paused, and stepped into the tiny hallway between the bedroom and sitting room. My heart began to beat faster, and I couldn't stop it, even with long breaths. My hands began to shake, not unlike Lizzie's had. I opened the door to the train platform, but when the train stopped, I let it go without getting on. I jumped down from the platform onto the tracks: tracks I didn't see on my walk home. Thinking, I turned left, towards the town, and began to follow the curving lines.

I walked for about an hour. I saw where I had disembarked the first time I rode the train back, when my button hadn't worked. I passed a big field, now growing winter wheat under a sky somewhat bluer than it had been earlier. Winter clouds passed overhead, flirting with the idea of snow. The track curved and curved, ever so slightly, around and around. I passed the high road; it was empty of cars and people. I passed the road that went to the boys' school, marked with solemn stone lions. I passed the village church: it too was empty. No one lingered after services or swept the walkway. I walked past trees and open spaces and kept to the rails, always curving. I realized that there was just one track, not one for each direction. There had to be a turning-house, I thought, where the train could turn around to go the other way. I walked. My lungs filled with sharp air, cold but not unpleasant. The girls would be jealous. It was a beautiful clear day, a day etched into being by winter's crispness. And then I stopped.

I was at a gate, which was locked. But on either side of the gate, a low stone wall had collapsed. I looked around and saw a train platform about thirty yards ahead, covered in crunchy autumn leaves. The sun lit it up and made it welcoming, comforting. Any moment now, a train would come. Across the road from the gate, a handful of pale stephanotis bloomed. I couldn't have handled poppies, although I am certain they were growing elsewhere that day. I gathered as many as I could, and stepped over the wall. I walked down a crumbling asphalt path that had long ago begun to blend with the grass to either side of it, and was now in shady places losing its place to moss. I stepped off to the right and stood before the newest cluster of headstones.

"So you've found us," said a voice behind my right shoulder. Margery. Myra emerged from the path to my left, coming from just out of the corner of my eye. I saw Theia playing ahead, where Alice tossed a stick for her.

"We forget," Myra said. "When we're on the train."

"The train goes in a circle, doesn't it?" I asked. "Both directions, but always just a circle."

"Hello, Janet," said Mary. Susan was coming up behind her in her big feathery hat.

"Yes," Myra said. "We... get on here, to travel to school, and while we do, we're still *there*, you see. But once we get to the academy, we remember, and the train keeps on. For you, the train goes both ways, doesn't it?"

"Yes," I said. "But only from a certain door does it go at all."

Alice came up, scratching Theia's ears. "I tried going the other way once," she said.

Mary seemed startled. "How did you do that?"

"I got on here, went to—someplace, I don't know—and got off. I crossed under the tracks and went to the other side, but the train never came. I must have waited days. Finally I did what we always have to do—I went back and got on going to school."

"But Helen can do it...?"

"No," said Susan. "We remember her going back and forth *then*, not now. Now she's the same as the rest of us. I think we were only able to go back that time because you were with us, Janet, and because you were taking us to some of our things, things we thought were lost."

They weren't exactly transparent, but the strong winter sunlight did pass through their uniforms and glossy hair. "I," I said, haltingly. "I brought you. Flowers."

"How thoughtful!" said Myra. She was holding Theia's leash. "Oh Janet, don't be upset."

"But Lizzie," I said, not quite asking, and starting to cry a little.

"I'm here," she said. She came up from my right. "I'm sorry I got so upset at your house," she said. She was curling her hair around her finger again. "I forgot. It was confusing, not being on the train but also not being here or at school."

"But look," she said, "We have a fine memorial, considering. And—" and she showed me their lovely headstones and a small memorial in the center of the cemetery, which gave their names and one other, and I put flowers all around. As we walked, Myra pulled me aside. "Lizzie forgets more," she said, "because her dress's ashes have not been placed here. Her dress is still at your flat."

"What about the other dress?"

"It didn't have an armband, did it? It belongs to someone who's not *here*."

The girls took me up to the platform later and we all rode the train. They saw me get off at my usual stop before the woods and waved merrily. We had been talking about Christmas parties and how to make the perfect hot toddy.

When Alice asked why I seemed sad and kept dabbing at my eyes, I told her I was going home soon, and would miss everyone.

"Oh, but you'll see us at Christmas," said Myra. "At the presentation."

And so I did.

But first I asked Mrs. Featherstone for a history of the town, and it turned out that there was one by a previous mayor, now sold from the mayor's office. Mrs. Featherstone and the Major were of an age to remember, and so one night over sherry in the lounge, I asked them about growing up here.

"The best place in all of England," said the Major. "We had everything: the military and girls' schools, best of the nation; solid industry; the rail system was top-notch, why we were going to be important—why, when I was at the boys' school, we had the very best education. Professors from Oxford and Cambridge and all over the world, and that's why the government chose us for the Project—"

I knew, by that point, about the Project.

Mrs. Featherstone took pity on me. "We were close enough to London, you see," she said," that their people could come and go on the regional rail. But we were far enough away that if something happened in the experiments, it wouldn't harm the people there. And of course nothing happened like that. But there was the air raid, and because no one knew what was going on here, and because they still can't know—even though the Project ended long ago—we won't get a nice memorial like Coventry, or be listed in books."

One of the top researchers in the country had come to the village in 1923. She was working on a method to end the Long War. While the men from the government worked on their portions of the Project at the boys' school, she had to maintain undercover by teaching at the girls' academy, and she also built her lab there. For quick travel and communications, they had the circular train line built, with a turning station between the two schools. She recruited nine of her best students to work with her in the lab, which was built underneath the school's sciences hall. The work of all the researchers and their student assistants—there were schoolboys involved, too—was top secret and highly dangerous. And there was an element of the occult as well, never fully explained. But when the school was closed in 1926 and most students moved to its temporary quarters farther north, Dr. Ford and her assistants stayed on. On Christmas Eve, Dr. Ford closed down the lab for a few days so that she and her girls could celebrate, and that night, eight of them dressed in their whites and prepared to accompany Dr. Ford to an event in town, where they would take part in the traditional Christmas presentation. Lizzie Davies, who had just recovered from the flu, volunteered to stay behind and keep an eye on things. They were killed instantly when the League targeted the site with its own new pinpoint weapon. When workers in protective suits went to the site for recovery, the bodies of the young women and their professor crumbled into ash as they were being placed in lead caskets. The immediate academy area was quarantined indefinitely, and the boys' school, which had been empty during Christmas week, was closed. The train was decommissioned, and its tracks removed; the government thought perhaps that aerial photography of the train and tracks had given away the researchers' positions. The prime minister would only say that the incident in the village was a boiler explosion and unrelated to war work. The school closed that year in its temporary place and never reopened. The Project remained secret, and is still classified.

  The Major was still talking. "And the Project is what gave us the best drinking water in all of Britain and the best milk from our cows, and let me also say that—"

  "That reminds me," said Mrs. Featherstone. "There's a woman in the village who has to check radiation or something out at the academy next week and she said if you promised not to touch anything and to wear one of those spaceman suits, you could go with her."

  We took a jeep, not a train, to the academy. We wore "spaceman" suits and while Dr. Heyward marked off paces and made readings from a machine and put orange-painted stakes into the ground at a number of points, I toured the grounds. It must have been a beautiful place to grow up and learn. The trees got denser before opening up onto a great lawn, which once had been carefully landscaped with a pond and trellis-growing plants. Wooden chairs, now fallen into splinters, had dotted the grass in pairs and threes and singly. The science hall was a dark space: a crater with edges softened by time and animals and nature, falling in on itself. I could just see a few shards of glass mixed with the soil. In places, the evidence of train tracks still poked through: lines of dead grass, and indentations. The platform had been removed, but it was obvious where it had been, underneath some oaks at the very bottom of the lawn. Some parts of the school still stood: a dormitory, with curtains in the cracked windows; the refectory, with a milk truck still in place from its delivery; a tennis court, broken through with weeds and birds' nests. The chapel was near collapse.

Dr. Heyward found me near an old asphalt trail. "That goes to a little graveyard," she said. "But it's actually pretty far. We haven't had to test out there for years. Only good thing about pinpoint technology: it really only contaminates a small area." I was relieved. She looked around. "It's a pretty place," she said. "Nature will take it back, and it'll be safe again."

For some, it was already safe again. I opened the door to the train platform from my flat for the last time on Christmas Eve, and the girls on the train were excited and laughing.

"What happens if I ride the train to school with you?" I asked. "Will I—get in trouble?"

Myra and Theia grinned at me. "No, not today, I'm sure," she said. "We're on holiday!"

So I stayed on the train as it passed the house where frost danced on the grass, and where the stream was beginning to freeze; and the villa, where I mused aloud that the girls should buy it and make it an artists' colony or something, to which Helen raised an eyebrow and looked thoughtful; and the edge of the woods, where I usually disembarked, where crepe paper in red and green had been strung up; and into the woods. A shadow came over the carriage, and the girls got quieter. Theia leaned her head against Myra's knee, and Mary stroked the dog's ears. Alice began arranging her bags around her: Christmas gifts threatened to fall out all over the car. Lizzie and Susan and other girls were humming a carol. No one asked what was in my bag. There were ten of us on the train.

The train slowed as it rounded the curve that would take us to the academy station; it slowed infinitely, to the slowest possible movement I thought I could imagine, and the girls' faces became grey, and their eyes widened and then closed tight, and they reached for each other's hands, and as we passed the stand of oaks that had sheltered the platform, there was a great sigh as though the wind had passed through the carriage, but there was no movement in the air, and they were gone. Ever so slowly the train labored on until it came near the cemetery station, and I pressed the button to stop. It glowed its familiar green.

Eight of them welcomed me at the station. They were in their whites. "How is this?" I asked. "Ghosts can wear whatever they want?"

"Pretty much," said Mary. "Although I don't think any of us—well, maybe Helen—are really comfortable with things out of our own time."

I looked around. Myra noticed. "Lizzie said she won't come out until she can wear her white with us," she said.

"Silly whites," said Helen, who was smoking a ghostly cigarette in a long holder. The ash fell as smoke to the ground. But she wore her white too.

"Are we ready?"

Shy Georgina, who had never been on the train when I was on it, led the way. We circled the space and drew a dress out of my bag. I held it up and brushed it off carefully, arranging the neckline just so, shaking out the creases. Together, we laid it down, and I lit a match.

If you have never burnt anything but charcoal or paper, you might be surprised by the way some things burn. The white burnt evenly, the fire moving from the edges to the center. The sleeves unraveled in a twist of smoke, and the dress became shorter even as the drapery of the top fell away to cinders. I stirred it into the soil with a spoon I'd taken from my flat, and laid new flowers. "It's done," said a voice new to the night, and there was Lizzie, with her classmates in her white gown. We marched around, giddy, putting fresh flowers down for everyone, even those beyond the nine.

"Where is Dr. Ford?" I asked, stopping suddenly at Myra's place.

"They sent her to her family," said Kirky. "But I think sometimes I've seen her here, just a flicker."

Julie nodded. "When the train passes by the hall," she said. "Sometimes she waves."

The morning came and the stars faded and the girls milled about, uncertain.

"What happens now?" I said. "Does anything change, now that Lizzie has her white and I know about you?"

"I don't think so," said Susan. "My cousin who visits knows too."

"I think we all just go on," said Mary. Alice threw a stick for Theia, and she shot out from underneath a tree to fetch it.

"I'll remember," I said.

"So will we," said Lizzie. "And we won't. But it's how it is."

Myra caught Theia around the middle as the dog ran back with her stick and gave her a hug.

"Happy Christmas," she said.

April Shade
Patricia Gomes

The ghost writes
lazily; she has nothing but time.
Time, dark windows, and echoing hallways.
Her not-quite-there pen hangs
in mid-air, balanced between long spectral fingers.
Lines form of spider silk, perfumed words,
protracted phrases as unhurried
as a graveyard snail traversing pine needles
and parched carnations.
A silverfish her companion, the moon her supper,
a stone slab for repose,
the ghost writes lazily,
enjoying the tomb-silence of her ever-after.

The Dead Have Ears
Greg Schwartz

The dead have ears
and they listen to us.
They listen to us
living and breathing
after their lives were snatched away
and they were stuffed in a box
underground, forgotten.
They listen with jealousy
that rots into anger.
They listen patiently
biding their time
as we stomp around above them
because really,
they have all the time
in the world.

Good Magic
Katherine Kerestman

. . . we shall find that the God of Israel is among us, when ten of us shall be able to resist a thousand of our enemies, when he shall make us a praise and glory, that men shall say of succeeding plantations: the Lord make us like that of New England: for we must consider that we shall be as a City upon a hill, the eyes of all people are upon us; so that if we deal falsely with our God in this work we have undertaken and to cause him to withdraw his present help from us, we shall be made a story and a by-word through the world, we shall open the mouths of enemies to speak evil of the ways of God, and all professors for God's sake. . .

    from *The Model of Christian Charity*, 1630
    John Winthrop, first Massachusetts Governor

    No. Victoria sat straight up and tapped her fingers on the table. She replaced the planchette on the Ouija board. The board was a souvenir of last autumn's New England vacation. *Every time I put my hands on it, it shoots over to "No."* Victoria often thought about that October day in Salem -- when she had placed her fingers upon an automatic writing planchette to which a pen was attached: the planchette had shot off the paper, trailing a line of blue ink all the way to the edge of the table, over which it had careened. Amazed, she had looked to the shopkeeper, but he had merely grinned and shrugged his shoulders. Wrinkling her forehead, Victoria repositioned herself, picked up the planchette, and replaced it on the Ouija board, and –

straightaway it slid to *No.* And then it moved to *Goodbye.*

***

On that vacation, she had fallen in love with Salem, a town which was -- three centuries after the witch trials -- still clothed in mourning. Victoria's own grief for the victims weighed so heavily upon her heart that she felt compelled to learn all that she could of their stories. You see, for people like Victoria, history is a living thing: *having existed* and *having spoken* and *having done* last forever. *Having been* is always present tense. It is true that certain people know this to be a fact. Therefore, when, in the pages of a magazine through which she was browsing in a waiting room, Victoria discovered a seventeenth-century house in Salem at auction, she did not waste a minute. Putting up her own house up for sale, she placed a bid on the historic dwelling. Six months later, she gave the key to her old house to the realtor and turned the key in the ignition of a U-Haul truck.

***

She toted the last box from the U-Haul, set it down in the grass, and sat down upon it, wishing to take a good look at her new home. A white frame house in the colonial cliché, its two stories of multi-paned windows were a study in symmetry. The entrance was surmounted by a triangular cornice, embellished by a groaning iron knocker, and flanked by many diminutive panes of wavy, leaded glass. Square timber columns demarcated the edges of the small porch, which was joined by a pebbly path to a tree-lined street, where the signs cautioned *Parking for Residents Only*, to ward off errant tourists. The limbs of the bare-branched trees reached above the roof and the chimney, whence more than a few fugitive bricks had absconded. The leaves -- the self-same leaves, which before the summer's demise, had hung on those branches, and had shrouded the house whenever the sun had attempted to shine on it -- lay dead now. Heaped up in layers upon the ground before the house, some crunched when trod upon, others were soft and wet. Unshrouded by the now-barren branches, the house stood revealed, whitewashed, and waiting. The house received her, and the door closed behind her. Later, the moving van would bring her furnishings.

***

Had Aurora herself peeped through the windows, she would have seen that, before dawn, Victoria had already made some headway in putting her home in order. By mid-day, the walls and floors had been washed and the cobwebs swept away -- and Victoria was scavenging for relics in the attic and root cellar (s*eek and ye shall find,* she hoped). Lo, in a crookedly hanging, musty old cupboard on the stone wall of the ancient cellar, she discovered a straw-filled poppet secreted within a Pandora's Box of assorted buttons. Wiping her dirty hands on her jeans, Victoria studied the archaic figure: chicken bones, which served as the doll's hands and feet, protruded from the delicate flaxen fabric.

The conquest of her wild demesne was the evening's task she had set herself; but, as she was pushing the lawnmower, it collided with an object concealed beneath the knee-high blades of grass. She turned off the engine and uncovered a pair of stones, which bore faint traces of skulls, and angel wings and difficult-to-read names and dates. Victoria's new life was off to an auspicious start! *"Tomorrow I shall work in the old carriage house next to –?"* she thought. "What is your name, ancient house?" she called out loud -- whereupon the wind began to blow hard and cold, a crack of thunder reverberated from the heavens, and Victoria felt the first drops of rain. *You have spoken your own name, Storm House,* she thought; and she dashed into the house to escape the now heavy downpour.

It was night when she drew a steaming bath in the claw foot tub and looked with appreciation upon the bead board molding and ancient fixtures of her creaky bathroom. It was after midnight, by the time she curled up in her wing chair in front of the brick fireplace and listened to the storm pummeling the old roof. Having done all that she could do in one day, she climbed the creaking stairs to bed. Nestled under fluffy comforters, she found contentment in the groaning of the old wood walls, and the tapping of the bare-branched trees on the roof of Storm House.

After breakfast, she was already walking the narrow lanes, which were rendered narrower yet by the rows of trees lining either side. Several of the trees stood naked in the autumn chill, having cast their raiments upon the grass and sidewalk; others were attired, still, in their fall finery of auburn and gold. All the elderly houses hemming the little streets seemed to call out *How Do You Do?* to their new neighbor. She turned her steps toward downtown Salem.

"So, you have taken Ezekial Trask's house," remarked the grizzled clerk at the town hall, and Victoria responded that she would be opening the Fountain of Youth in the carriage house on her property. The clerk guided Victoria in completing the paperwork, accepted her check, and wished her well. After she ordered brochures from the printer in the next building, Victoria resumed her progress down the street.

She entered a witchery next, where -- over the counter which was jumbled with quartzes and crystals -- she chatted with the garrulous blonde proprietress, Peony. The vivacious purveyor of herbs and crystal balls assured Victoria that her shop would fill a vacant niche in the Salem market. She bent to pick up the yellow and white tomcat who was rubbing her leg; and she introduced Honeysuckle to Salem's newest citizen: "Watch over her, Honeysuckle. She needs some friends now." Honeysuckle purred.

When their conversation shifted to the history of Salem, Victoria confessed the sorrow she felt for the victims of 1692, whereupon Peony offered, "Perhaps you are one of those unfortunate souls, reincarnated." Victoria smiled, not knowing the proper way to respond to such a curious suggestion, and inquired whether Peony knew where the accused witches had been hanged – her research had failed to pinpoint Gallows Hill on a map. Peony explained that Gallows Hill is a small park tucked in a residential area; she jotted directions on a notepad.

The new shopkeeper spent the remainder of her day unpacking and arranging her wares, and transforming the erstwhile carriage house into a luxurious retreat. The painters had been hard at work there since morning; and when afternoon passed into evening, they loaded their drop cloths and ladders into their van. Victoria thanked the workmen, and then she looked upon her shop with pride. Delicate white eyelet curtains fluttered prettily, in the breeze from the open window, and a mauve slipper chair beckoned invitingly; beside it, a full-length mirror on an antiqued-white easel reflected the points of light from the small crystal chandelier. Lavender lotions and bath salts were arrayed upon old-fashioned tables covered with white lace cloths. Gold-edged placards on the shelf of a French armoire announced that a product line called *Timeless* was created with early morning dew and that the *Countess Bathory Eternal Youth* emollient was made from cruelty-free virgin blood (voluntarily donated at a hygienic blood bank). *Love Potion No. 666* was given a prominent place in the window. It was night now, and Victoria turned out the lights; through the open door she could see twinkling constellations sprinkled among the white clouds, which were softly lit by the moon. A black cat strode in and sprang upon the counter.

"Moonbeam!" Victoria exclaimed, as she picked him up. Of her new friend's name, she had not a doubt. She fastened the door, and Moonbeam trotted after her to Storm House.

***

On the day of her Grand Opening, Victoria welcomed dozens of customers, who sampled her apple cider and spiced cookies, tried on her lotions and fragrances, and wished her good luck -- while Moonbeam gamboled about the balloons and streamers and endeared himself to the ladies who vied to hold him. At the end of the workday, Victoria rode Broomstick (her bicycle) to search out Gallows Hill. For half an hour, she pedaled through a labyrinth of small lanes, until she spotted a modest stone marker, to which was affixed a small brass plate engraved with the words "Gallows Hill Park." Dismounting, she propped Broomstick against a great tree; and she rambled about the desolate park, lost in solemn meditation upon its cruel history.

When she was ready to return home, she raised her eyes to find Broomstick – only to discover that she was standing at the periphery of a noisy throng – a bewildering assembly of women clad in brown and black dresses with wide white collars and aprons, men wearing short breeches with buckled hats and shoes -- and horses and wagons! She hid herself behind a prodigious tree, and, from her place of concealment, she witnessed a horrific scene: a woman, corralled by an uncouth mob, was engaged in a desperate struggle for her life -- *two men were binding her hands and placing a noose around her neck!* Over the din, Victoria heard the woman shouting – her words directed to the minister on horseback -- "I am no more a witch than you are a wizard. And if you take away my life, God will give you blood to drink!" Victoria heard the sickening thud -- as the woman was dropped, and hanged by the neck until she died.

When she opened her eyes, she was lying sprawled atop the blanket of decomposing leaves covering the sodden pasture; and the moon had risen to assume its position in the starless sky. Hastily retrieving Broomstick from the place she had left her -- the hanging tree – she returned to Storm House, utterly incapable of even attempting to put a name to her terrifying experience. It was not until she was sheltered within the depths of the great wing chair before her hearth, staring into the yellow flames, that she could face the question of whether she had had a dream, or, perhaps, a vision. *Those poor people,* she repeated to herself from time to time that evening, until she went to bed. *Those poor people.* Moonbeam remained by her side all through the night.

***

While Moonbeam prowled for chipmunks the next morning, Victoria inspected the tombstones on her lawn. The two hoary slabs were leaning lopsided in the soil, as though they were fatigued; indeed, they had borne piteous injuries. Their abraded corners were crumbling, their skulls had been fractured, and their angel wings lacerated. *Ezekial Trask 1642— 1692,* the chiseled characters on the first stone spelled, *Martha, wife of Ezekial Trask 1664-1688,* the second, the disintegrating letters of their lives nearly scoured away by the winds and tempests of three hundred years. Victoria returned to the house for a bucket of water and a brush, with which she tenderly cleaned the stones.

Evelyn Drake, the president of the Historical Society, was her second customer that day. The genial historian cordially accepted a cup of Victoria's pumpkin spice coffee; and then, placing her cup and saucer on the counter, she told her about the Trasks. Martha Trask had perished in childbirth, she said; her daughter, Rebekkah, had been stillborn; and Goodman Trask had been accused of witchcraft. Trask's accusers had alleged that -- although he was crippled and bedbound and had to be fed his gruel from a spoon -- still he sent his spirit forth to torment them in their beds. In the end, he had cheated the hangman by dying in his sleep the night before he was to have been arrested, yet the Reverend Parris excommunicated him posthumously and forbade his burial in Christian soil -- and that was how he had come to be buried in Victoria's front yard. Victoria's eyes were glistening; Moonbeam wound his way between Victoria's ankles.

***

The next day, Victoria hung a hand-lettered sign upon the door of the carriage house, stating, "Sorry, We are Closed Today. Please Come Back Tomorrow," and she drove to Boston, where she spent the morning hours roaming the portrait galleries and the period rooms of the Fine Arts Museum. After lunch, she followed the yellow bricks of the Freedom Trail, which led her past the Old North Church and the Bunker Hill obelisk to Copp's Hill Burying Ground. There -- in the corner most distant from the entrance -- she was confronted with the brick, altar-shaped tomb of the Mather family.

Oh, did she let them have it, in her thoughts --at least, she did not think she had spoken the words aloud-- for she knew that *the Mathers, father and son, had supplied the ideology, authority, and mandate that allowed the inquisitors to arrest, sentence, and kill their neighbors! They had instigated, and had given credibility to, a holocaust of innocents! Incited by cruel doctrine, the murderers had styled themselves knights-in-arms in a holy war against Satan! Thereby, perished men, women, and children who were sincere Christian folk! Thereafter, descended a shroud of sorrow over Salem, always palpable, even to this day!*

Preoccupied with these thoughts, Victoria did not immediately notice the lean black cat who had silently appeared upon the Mather grave, upon which she, too, had been standing. The bewhiskered interloper crossed the graveyard, from that lonesome corner where the Mathers rested, to the gate at the main entrance -- pausing occasionally to groom herself, and resolutely resisting each tourist who beckoned *Kitty, Kitty*. Somehow, Victoria knew that the feline had come to watch over her; and she feared that she might, indeed, have need of a protector -- for, as she departed the Mathers' tomb, she became aware of an icy chill prickling her skin.

She departed Copp's Hill, anxious now to return to the comfort of Storm House -- but, when her car reached the end of the entrance ramp and merged with the lateral lane of Route 95, she became caught up in a quagmire of vehicles that nearly prohibited movement -- and then, following several hours of driving through what seemed more quicksand than asphalt, she overshot her exit and lost her way, prolonging her journey by two additional hours. When she arrived at Storm House, she was quite exasperated. She tossed her coat onto the table in the foyer and sank, exhausted, into her chair before the fire, where, brushing Moonbeam's velvety coat, she pondered the unsettling possibility that Cotton and Increase Mather might have had something to do with her misadventures on the road.

***

Victoria's customers, the next morning, were desirous of knowing whether the secret to eternal youth could truly be found among the bottles and jars on her shelves -- and when she demonstrated the wonders of her masques and moisturizers, they were one and all astounded by the results. In the afternoon, Peony dropped in, both to admire her colleague's boutique and to invite Victoria to a séance at Ouija, her own establishment; intrigued, Victoria accepted.

Bearing a bouquet of lavender, she arrived at Ouija at dusk, and Peony showed her into the meeting room. Victoria was delighted to see Evelyn Drake among the company and pleased to make the acquaintance of Ronald and Jessica Brown, sibling librarians at the university. Once they had saluted one another's health with honeyed mead, Evelyn lowered the lights and cast a magic circle. Peony indicated to Victoria where she should sit, and her friends assumed their accustomed places. On the top of the Hepplewhite table, in the center of which a black taper was flickering in a pewter candle holder, they placed their palms so that their fingers were touching. As Evelyn was whispering, "This candlestick was made by Paul Revere," the door flew open with a violent clatter that caused them all to jump in their seats.

Arctic gusts invaded the room, flapped the velvet draperies, and extinguished the candle. A photo fell from the wall, the glass breaking in the frame. The dark chamber began to glow with a weird crimson light.

"Die, Witch!" a deep male voice thundered from the shadows.

Victoria pushed back her chair, rose, and spoke to the darkness: "Devil in a parson's skin, Avaunt!" The red glow faded. All eyes were on Victoria, and she stared back at them.

When she arrived home, Victoria laid sprigs of lavender upon the graves of Ezekial and Martha Trask. Her sleep was restless – for it was fraught with flashbacks of the hanging on Gallows Hill.

***

In the morning, when she arrived to open her shop, she discovered four of her favorite clients waiting for her; and with a warm smile, she opened the doors to let them in. And then Ronald and Jessica Brown came up the walk; Victoria pulled them to the side and whispered: "That was my first séance, and I find myself quite at a loss for words!"

"We came here to ask you how long you have been practicing witchcraft," responded Jessica, "and to invite you to meet our coven."

"I am so very sorry if I have given the wrong impression. I'm not a witch."

"My dear, you *are*, in fact, a powerful witch -- your exorcism of the evil spirit at the séance last night proved so," insisted Ronald. Jessica nodded in agreement.

"The only explanation I can offer for my behavior," Victoria explained, "is that the voice we heard at the séance reminded me of Cotton and Increase Mather—I visited their tomb when I was in Boston two days ago. Their pride and cruelty destroyed so many lives --" she inhaled sharply and balled her hands into fists at her sides "– that I am incensed whenever I think about those men!"

"Your denunciation of the Mathers upon their grave, dear Victoria, has set in motion the events that brought you here to Salem."

"I have always felt that past and present were one," Victoria considered.

"Perhaps you were summoned here for that reason."

***

The balance of the week passed without incident, and Victoria questioned whether the strange occurrences of late were simply an illusion born of her elation at moving to a seventeenth-century house in Salem and immersing herself in the lore of the witch trials. Her business was flourishing, and she felt that several women had enhanced their appearances with regular use of her products. She had received many compliments about the "magic" she was working.

Halloween was approaching, and the weekends saw wonderful incursions of tourists.

One fine evening, Victoria was sitting upon an ornately carved bench in the Colonial Garden at The House of the Seven Gables, gazing with admiration upon the sapphire waves rippling in the harbor. This celebrated house had been the setting for Nathaniel Hawthorne's novel of the same name; Hawthorne, sorely burdened by familial guilt, had endeavored, through his literature, to make amends for his ancestor's complicity in the witch trials. He was Victoria's favorite writer.

In pain and surprise, Victoria cried out – she had been knocked into the flower bed by a tall, red-haired man, just as a large branch crashed with a bang, creating a crack in the concrete bench upon which she had been sitting! She leapt to her feet – and just one glance was sufficient for her to realize that the red-haired man had just saved her life.

"How can I ever thank you?" she asked, pushing her skewed coif from her eyes, and dusting the mulch from her knees.

With a bow, the gallant man replied, "The pleasure is mine, fair lady -- although, I must confess, I am tempted to inquire whose wrath you have incurred."

"Come now, are you really implying that there is more to this than my simply being in the wrong place at the wrong time?" she asked, confused by his remark.

The man waved his hand toward the tree: "The branch is green, the trunk is healthy, and there is no wind," and Victoria was obliged to agree with him. Museum employees arrived and asked if she were all right. Victoria assured them that she was uninjured, and she accepted her rescuer's invitation to raise a glass to her narrow escape at the Tarot Card Café, across the street.

His name was Philip Corey. Not one of *the* Corey's? asked Victoria. Philip told her that he taught history at Salem State University. And, yes, he was a descendent of that irascible old man who would not give them the satisfaction. Victoria knew the story of Giles Corey who, in an effort to forestall the seizure of his property, had refused to enter a plea of innocence or guilt to the charge of witchcraft. Giles was pressed to death --tortured by the weight of the stones that crushed the life out of him – and his legendary last words were, "More weight." Victoria confided to Philip that she had always felt a connection with Salem and that she had recently moved into the old Ezekial Trask house. Trask would not give them what they wanted, either, she said: he died in his own bed before they came for him. The pair lingered in the tavern for dinner.

***

Halloween was imminent -- "Thriller" was playing on the radio, and Moonbeam, sitting upon the counter, was intently observing Victoria, who was plunging a knife into a pumpkin and transforming it into a Jack-o-Lantern. The cat leapt suddenly from the counter -- just as a man appeared in the doorway. The stranger looked a lot like a shadow, for he was dressed all in black—even his moustache was ebony as nightfall. His beard concluded in a sharp point and curled up at the end -- but it was the abyss of his eyes that struck Victoria. Extending a gnarled finger, the weird man groaned, "Desist, woman, lest thou rue thy meddling!" – and before Victoria could close her gaping mouth, he was gone. She dashed to the door, peered out into the street, the pumpkin knife still clenched in her white-knuckled fingers —

but the apparition had vanished! Victoria closed her shop and went home, Moonbeam close by her heels.

On her way home, Victoria gathered an armful of logs from the woodpile; she brought them inside, and stacked them next to the hearth, endeavoring to focus her mind on her task. But she found herself powerless to exorcise the image of the vile trespasser. The jangling of the telephone jolted her from her fugue – it was Peony, calling to warn her that she had sensed peril. Learning of the weird stranger, the enchantress directed Victoria to trace a pentacle in the earth around the house and to position lanterns in all of its five corners. Accepting the sorceress's peculiar advice, Victoria went out into the twilight; she used a green stick to draw a five-pointed star in the dirt, hopeful that the talisman would provide sufficient protection to Storm House and those within.

When she re-entered the house, her thoughts returned, as they were wont, to the witch trials; and she reached for the venerable tome that lay on the table, to revisit the woeful story. As she turned the pages to the chapter that described Cotton and Increase Mather's roles in the holocaust, the wind began to wail. A maniacal churning of the leaves outside the window foretold a tempest. Slashes of lightning divided the blackness -- and then torrents of rain extinguished the lanterns in the corners of her recently constructed pentagram.

Victoria hurried to the telephone when it rang again. This time Philip was on the line, inviting her to view *The History of Halloween,* a documentary, at the Salem Cinema. Thankful for his well-timed invitation, she ascended the stairs to dress. When she spied the poppet on her bed, she tucked it into her handbag on an impulse. A short time later, as she opened the door to Philip, she was pleased to see that the storm had ended -- although his observation that, despite the crackling fire, the house had the chill of the grave concerned her.

Following the movie, they strolled the leaf-strewn, moonlit lanes of Salem, each pointing out to the other the landmarks they recognized. When they reached Howard Street, they followed the chain-link fence to the entrance of the burying ground, which had been the site of Giles Corey's pressing. Opening the gate for Victoria, Philip spoke proudly of his ancestor -- and the nineteen victims who had died by hanging because they had refused to plead guilty (a false confession of guilt was the only means by which an accused person could avoid execution). Philip had high regard for people who would not compromise their integrity.

"This was not a graveyard in 1692 --"

He collapsed, on the grassy mound of a century-old grave.

"Call 911!" Victoria shouted to the tourists outside the fence -- while she checked Philip for signs of life. Although his skin was cool and moist -- *he was breathing*! Victoria tried to comfort him, not knowing whether he could hear her. The howling of the approaching ambulance gave her hope; and she remained with Philip until the ambulance conveyed him to the hospital.

When she learned of Philip's plight, Peony declared that it was time to close ranks -- and Victoria readily agreed. So, at ten o'clock, Peony closed Ouija and pulled the shades, explaining to Victoria that she would open the door only to those who knocked in the coven sign of three slow knocks. When her twelve guests arrived, they arrayed themselves in small clusters; and Peony circulated among them, bearing a silver tray laden with spiced wine in curious goblets that were wreathed with pentacles and moons. She introduced Victoria to her associates and brought them up to date on Victoria's strong emotional connection to the departed victims of 1692, as well as her acquisition of the Ezekial Trask homestead, her vision at Gallows Hill, the familiar at the Mathers' grave, and the ill fortune that had followed her back from Boston. At Peony's behest, Victoria told them about the séance. When she had finished her account, Ronald Brown came forward and took her hands in both of his own, saying earnestly, "Dear Victoria, surely you must be aware by now that you are one of the innocents returned." Victoria told Peony's friends that Philip had saved her from the falling branch -- of his collapse in the Howard Street Burial Ground -- of the menacing intruder who had cursed her in her shop.

There was an excited outcry among her auditors, all of them speaking at once. Everyone agreed that the evil which had put Salem on the map had returned! In 1692, living men and women -- with pious words in their mouths and hatred in their bosoms -- had murdered their own neighbors—and now, with one foot in the Present and one foot in the Past, Victoria had stood upon the graves of Cotton and Increase Mather and reviled the father and son for the suffering and death which they had caused. Clearly, as Victoria had rebuked them on their blood-soaked graves, the Mathers' spirits had been roused! Alfred P. Potsworth, senior docent at one of the witch museums, recommended an exorcism. Morgan Ellsworth, concierge at the historic hotel, urged them to consider setting a trap with a dark mirror. Josephine (no last name) said that she believed they could work an efficient spell with graveyard dirt and war water sprinkled over the Mather tomb.

Amid the commotion, no one noticed that Victoria was cowering on the floor. When Morgan spied her in an empty corner of the dim chamber, she whispered to Peony, who moved swiftly to kneel at her side.

"Dear, whatever is the matter? Are you frightened?" she asked, clasping her hands before her.

Gazing at the floor, Victoria stammered, "Mama! Mama! Where are you, Mama? My poppet. Poppet."

"Who is your Mama, child?" urged Peony.

"Goody Good," came the timorous reply. "My poppet. Prithee, Good Sir, canst thou take the iron off? I cannot move my legs. I did not mean to be a witch."

They were witnessing the rebirth of Dorothy -- the four-year old daughter of Sarah Good. Dorothy grew up insane and required a keeper all her life – for she had lived eight months of her fifth year of life in chains.

All through the night, Peony remained with Victoria, cradling her in her arms; and, when she at last awakened, Peony described the trance for her, for her friend had no memory of it. At long last, Victoria was able to understand her preoccupation with Salem – and why, all her life, she had cringed when one party claimed superiority over another -- how such attitudes had always terrified her! This new awareness of her legacy strengthened Victoria's resolve to drive the wicked souls of the Mathers back to the fire.

***

Finding it impossible to concentrate on her work the next day, she was relieved when Philip called to tell her that he was to be released from the hospital in the afternoon; and they arranged to meet for dinner at a restaurant on the waterfront. That evening, when Victoria perused the restaurant from the doorway, she spied a beaming Philip beckoning from a candlelit table. Crossing the busy room, she noted with approval the fishnets and captain's wheels adorning the walls and the picture window that offered a view of the boat-laden docks. A silver ice bucket on their table held a bottle of a local vintage, a witch riding a broomstick before a round yellow moon on its label. Philip pulled out a chair for her, and then he poured two full glasses and handed one to Victoria.

She had just begun to express her bewilderment at the doctors' lack of a diagnosis, when Philip interrupted: "I was being pressed to death. I could not breathe. The weight—Oh, God, it was excruciating! I could not remember, and then. . . I started to remember." He drained the golden wine in a long gulp and then set the stem glass down hard upon the table. Victoria reached for it to keep it from spilling.

"Philip, Giles Corey is alive in you! I think I know who I am, too!"

After dinner, they walked across town to Ouija, for they had decided to seek counsel from Peony. Their path was necessarily circuitous -- for the narrow thoroughfares of the old town were teeming with euphoric tourists. The pair walked quickly, past the police cars -- on whose doors witches on broomsticks soar above the logo "Witch City" -- and past the policemen -- who were providing directions to the legions of excited visitors. They hurried past the doomsaying fellow, who (from his usual position at the confluence of Washington and Essex Streets) was tendering his annual holiday greeting (somewhat dire tidings of fire and brimstone). They noted the signs carried by some in the crowd, on which were lettered grim reminders that self-righteousness, such as his, had brought Salem to its knees in 1692.

"Witch, thou shalt perish!"-- the resounding threat seemed to come from the loudspeaker – *"Thou shalt repent thy return!"*

Pulling Victoria by the hand, Philip flew toward the evangelist with the bullhorn -- he was sitting on a park bench, sharing coffee and his religious views with a television reporter from Boston. Philip queried many people in the square, but none other than they had heard anything alarming. Mystified, the pair hastened to Ouija.

The aisles of Peony's store were packed with excited people in Halloween costumes, and the clerks were hard at work at the cash registers. Jostling their way through the crowd to the meeting room, Philip and Victoria found Ronald Brown addressing the coven:

"The vile legacy of Cotton and Increase Mather is returned. In 1692, the Mathers provoked foul feelings of envy and discord among the Puritans. The Mather poison turned neighbor against neighbor and obliterated conscience in Salem! Murder, libel, perjury, torture, and destitution they wrought-- in the name of God! Unable to heal the wounds, nor return the dead to life, at last the people of modern Salem have come to feel sorrow and shame – and we will not rest until we have banished the specter of 1692 to the past!"

Morgan added, "The return of two of the victims, now reincarnated as Victoria and Philip --and Victoria's denunciation upon their grave --have provoked the Mathers to spread conflict and doom in our own time."

"Witches are celebrated here," Jessica Brown interjected: "Modern Salem is *Witch City;* and witchery conjures reverence for everyone's Constitutional and human rights. "

"The Mathers' evil has come to a changed Salem -- a Salem which encourages individuality and denounces compulsory conformity!" added Peony, her fist raised in the air. "Good will may have been scarce in 1692, but compassion shall triumph in the present."

"On All Hallows Eve, the Witches' Circle will form in Salem Commons. People of many faiths will gather to celebrate with us," Alfred P. Potsworth reminded the friends. "Bred in a land defiled by the birthright of neighbor against neighbor, the people of Salem have learned the lesson of the past –" his voice swelling, "and *we desire never to repeat it.*"

"So mote it be," replied the congregation.

When the rest had gone, Victoria remained behind with Peony and Philip: *"Such unspeakable anguish – I cannot stand idle as the evil of the Mather legacy is resurrected! We must stop them!"* she cried, putting head in her hands.

"What a heroine you would have been little Dorothy," said Peony, touching her cheek, "had you been permitted to grow up without torture and chains. Reborn in this century, you are a virtuous and strong woman who will do as much good in this time as your tormentor wrought evil in your previous life."

"Giles learned courage late in life, but now that he is alive again in me -- *we are on a roll!*" added Philip, and the three clinked their goblets.

***

Business was brisk in the Fountain of Youth throughout the day on October 30. Throngs of tourists, in a last-minute shopping frenzy, had formed a queue outside the door, while inside her boutique Victoria demonstrated her lotions. As she offered handfuls of candy corn from a cast iron bowl fashioned like a miniature cauldron, she invited her clients to join the Witches' Circle in the Salem Commons. When her customers would ask her to tell them about *Samhain*, she would explain that, in the harvest season, when the realms of the living and the dead are closest, passing between them becomes easier; thus, at Samhain, many people try to communicate with those who have journeyed beyond this life. Yes, she assured her curious customers, some of the witches offer séances and instruction in conjuring.

At ten o'clock, Victoria closed her shop and tallied her sales, satisfied with the profits of her first season. Having deposited the day's receipts into the safe, she turned toward the door to leave. She gasped -- the diabolical man was there! His malevolent glare, razor-like, threatened to flay her soul into tatters! The crisp autumnal air soured -- and time skidded to a halt. As the boutique dissolved, Victoria found herself in a moldy, damp, and cold, stone dungeon. She strove to move her legs -- they were weighted with irons -- she bent to touch the heavy links.

"Quit thy whimpering, brat, or thou shalt see worse," the demon snarled.

Victoria felt a cyclonic wind dragging her into a brutal past.

"No!" burst from the paralysis that had seized her throat. "No! You will not have the child again." Flames erupted, the fire alarm shrieked -- and concerned pedestrians pulled on the locked door. Victoria seized the fire extinguisher from behind the counter and aimed the nozzle at the blaze. When the firemen arrived, they found evidence of a fire in a trash can; little damage had been done. Hugging her knees to her chest, Victoria huddled in the chintz chair; she knew that Philip was on his way to take her to Ouija.

***

As the witches at Ouija hovered protectively about Victoria, Josephine lit the candles and Ronald ignited the incense in the cauldron; and then each person contributed a drop of blood into the smoking reservoir. Tracing a magical circle with a jeweled wand -- while reciting arcane incantations -- Peony bade her congregation to petition the aid of departed loved ones. Victoria thought of her parents, who had been killed by a driver who was texting on her cell phone, on their way to her college graduation; she also remembered Goody Good -- the mother of her reincarnated self, four-year old Dorothy -- both Sarah Good and her infant had perished in the holocaust. Josephine declared:

"Good and evil are known by myriad names. Call upon goodness by whatever name you wish. The morrow being Samhain, we expect the Mathers to bring the crisis to the present."

The incense was heady, in the close, dark room. Victoria, Philip, and the coven of thirteen could feel their power. They were ready to meet the Mathers.

***

Victoria's quiet, tree-lined street was usually tranquil as death at dawn; but, as she stretched her arm out from the warren of bedclothes to silence the alarm clock on Halloween morning, Victoria could hear people coming -- by the busload.

Salem is a joyful town at Halloween. The historic graveyards, The House of the Seven Gables, and the house of Magistrate Corwin (the infamous brother of Sheriff Corwin, who used his cane to push Giles Corey's protruding tongue back into his mouth moments before his last breath was crushed out of him) are spaces consecrated to our collective remembrance of the horror of 1692 – but the costume balls, carnival games, and midway rides conjure a celebratory spell, a jubilant rejection of self-righteousness and death, and an exuberant embracing of empathy and life. Modern Salem's Halloween celebrates the fact that we have learned from the past. The air is charged with psychic energy.

Victoria emerged blithely from her warm and comfortable four-poster and started the coffee maker; and then she stepped into the shower, humming "Monster Mash." When she had toweled herself dry, she donned her blue chenille robe and stepped toward the mirror to complete her toilette – but, as she started to pull the comb through her hair, she was puzzled by the red spots she saw in the mirror. She turned to see what was being reflected.

"Oh, no!" she cried.

Frantic, she turned the antique handles in the old shower –in a futile effort to stop the dripping of the blood from the shower head: thick red clots of gore were dripping where she had only moments ago enjoyed a refreshing shower! She tried to wash the blood from her hands -- but blood was now oozing from the mirror, crimson viscous blood spilling down the silvery glass, in long rivulets, and then continuing, drop by drop, into the sink.

Clad only in her blue robe, and with water dripping from her hair, Victoria fled barefoot down the stairs, scooped up the keys to the carriage house, and rushed out the front door, leaving it wide open in her wake. She leapt off the stoop and saw congealing blood spurting from the gravestones. Kicking up the leaves, she sprinted across the lawn to the carriage house. Her hands trembled as she fumbled with the lock. She opened the door, slammed it shut again, and relocked it. Out of breath, she rang Peony.

"Oh, honey, how utterly dreadful for you! Have no doubt that you will be triumphant. Those accursed spirits have, by their repeated attempts to frighten you away, demonstrated that they know you for an adversary. By these tricks of theirs, they testify to your power -- power which you yourself have not yet recognized, my dear." Peony called for a council of war at the Rebecca Nurse Homestead, to prepare for the impending battle.

Victoria returned to Storm House, to dress and to collect Moonbeam. She no longer saw any blood on the headstones, as she stepped around them. Warily, she passed through the front door. Cautiously, she ascended the stairs to the creaky old bathroom, where she saw the towels which had been tossed on the floor and the cosmetics that she had abandoned on the sink, but the blood was gone there, too. Neither did the shower still drip blood, nor was there a drop of blood in the claw foot tub. Over her head Victoria slipped a black velvet witch's cowl, with elongated sleeves and a hem that skimmed the ground. She tinted her lips carmine, fastened a silver pentacle on a chain around her neck, and beckoned to Moonbeam to follow her to her shop. After locking the door, the witch and her familiar went to work.

The streets of Salem had been jam-packed for hours before Victoria opened her store, and a long line of strange and beautiful creatures stretched down the sidewalk from The Fountain of Youth: scores of women, fantastically appareled as the *Hocus Pocus* witches and Brides of Frankenstein, Scarlett O'Hara's and Marie Antoinette's, Hester Prynne's and Morticia Adams's, frightful ghosts and grisly zombies, were awaiting Victoria's magic to make themselves even more alluring for the masquerade balls. Applying her products liberally for her eager clients and seeing them off with laden shopping bags -- Victoria worked her magic.

***

In the late afternoon, Philip's car crunched along the dirt and gravel drive leading to the big red house that stands gravely on the left, atop a rolling green hill, the house from which Nurse had been dragged out of her sickbed to stand trial as a witch. The big red house – with its additions at odd angles tacked on over the years -- stands a grim testament to the blood of good people that soaked the land in 1692, when the farms went fallow – because hundreds of villagers languished in jail instead of working their fields. On the right is the meeting house, a facsimile of the real building in which

Reverend Samuel Parris encouraged his parishioners to cry *Witch* against one another.

The thirteen whom Victoria and Philip had come to meet were congregated at the burial ground beyond the house. Rebecca Nurse is said to be buried here; her body, stolen by her family from its shallow grave, was brought home. George Jacobs's body was also moved here from its original grave; he was ninety-one when he was hanged as a witch. Here, Danvers -- known, in 1692, as Salem Village -- has set up a memorial to a time when wicked men were in control and many others stood silent. The air is powerful. The soil is rich in martyrs' blood; it is a good place for a council. The fifteen arranged themselves in a circle and joined their hands. Peony began, "The most pressing matter is the safety of the witches and visitors who will be gathered in harmony this night."

"Let's each take a post in Salem Town, to put out stray embers of ill will and prevent the Mathers from igniting a conflagration," proposed Jessica.

Morgan suggested that they sweep from the edges of town toward the center, and then join the Witches' Circle. Alfred P. Potsworth advised the distribution of a draught for serenity to those gathered in the Commons. Victoria said that she wished to encourage the peace that was already present in the human heart, and Philip agreed with her: "All people have a natural conscience, which we must call upon tonight. It's vital that regular folks see for themselves that we all possess the power of goodness!"

All having assented, and their positions allocated, they had just started back through the graveyard toward their cars, when the wind began to roar, whipping up the dust and whirling the leaves about their feet. Hearing a commotion, Philip pulled Victoria close. A rumble in the distance was rapidly increasing to a deafening din -- and they could see dozens of great, black dogs, with fiery red eyes, and powerful, gnashing jaws, that opened to reveal sharp teeth, coming toward them! As the distance between themselves and the hounds closed, they could see the saliva dripping from the mouths of the beasts, their lips curling back, their ears flattened. The dogs came pounding over the driveway, over the grass, heading for our heroes. There was nowhere for them to run! The buildings were locked, and only meadow and woods surrounded them. The friends huddled, in imminent danger of being torn to pieces.

Victoria cried, "Familiars! Dear friends! Come to our aid! Deliver us from the hounds of hell!"

The beasts closing in, the council decided to make a run for their automobiles, but -- before they could reach their vehicles -- bloodcurdling howling rent the air. Moonbeam, Honeysuckle, the black cat from Copp's Hill Burying Ground, and hundreds of cats, rats, and owls were tearing the eyes out of the hell hounds, sinking their teeth and claws into their hides, riding astride the foul, possessed beasts, and spilling their blood! Amid the fray, Victoria espied Princess, her tortoiseshell cat who had passed on ten years before, and for whom she had mourned ever since, for the woman and cat had loved each other so very much. Victoria shed grateful tears, realizing that Princess had been loving her and watching over her all that time; she was thankful to have known such love, love which had survived even death.

A deep and gaping hole opened in the earth, from which sulfur and fumes arose; flickering fire was seen down, down very deep. The army of cats, rats, and owls drove the hounds of hell into the pit -- which swallowed them whole and closed upon them, leaving no sign of the earth having opened. Princess walked wearily toward Victoria, who gathered her in her arms. They gently kissed each other. Then

Princess jumped to the ground and walked off with the other familiars until they disappeared from Victoria's sight.

***

Back in Salem, the fifteen warriors deployed to their designated posts and then began their march toward the Commons. When he overheard the word "terrorist," mild-mannered Alfred P. Potsworth jumped into the fray, calming a disagreement over a parking space between a Caucasian man and a man of Middle Eastern descent, who, dressed as Aladdin, was carrying a rolled-up magic carpet under his arm; Alfred's affable manner ended in the men shaking hands. Jessica wished *Blessed Samhain* to a policewoman and a young African American man who were eyeing each other doubtfully; her gentle words had a mollifying effect, and they began to chat companionably, while the young man awaited his sweetheart, who was in the ladies' room donning her costume.

Nowadays, there is a great deal more good will than ill will in Salem, so there was little to detain the fifteen as they made their way to the Salem Commons, where the Witch Circle had already formed. Thousands of participants greatly enlarged the circle, near to filling the park, while thousands more packed the streets and shops in every conceivable costume. On this feast they remembered that neighbor had cried *Witch* against neighbor and had destroyed each other in 1692.

The huge, cheerful throng had formed a deep circle around the drummers and the witch leaders. The celebrants summoned the spirits of the four cardinal directions. They called on the elements of air, fire, water, and earth. They called for the celebration of the dead. They danced, a stomping, aboriginal type of step, to the beat of the drums and tambourines. As the dancing grew faster, the psychic energy was intensified. Gradually, the people in the outer circle began to join in. They whirled and stomped in a happy, increasing frenzy. Some tourists took photos of each other dancing. A frenetic hour had passed, and the witches in the center had given their blessing when people began to turn around and think about making their way to the balls or the party in the streets.

One and all were astounded to see that a circle -- three rings deep -- had been formed around their own circle. Cats, rats, owls, and dogs had formed a circle -- three rings deep -- their backs to the witches and friends -- thousands of creatures in a strange league, facing outward, to protect the dancers from attack by the hounds of hell, or any other weapon of the Mathers.

"All Nature cries out against cruelty and evil! We cast the demons in clerical habit back to the Prince of Darkness! They are not welcome in Salem anymore!" cried Victoria, who had made her way to the center and taken the microphone.

A great cheer arose from the crowd. Falling stars lit up the sky. Although there was no rain, it was later learned that lightning shattered the Mather Monument in Copp's Hill Burying Ground at the same exact moment. The start of the fireworks kicked off the evening festivities. And the cats, rats, owls, and dogs, one and all, trotted off to their homes. And the stern face on the statue of Nathaniel Hawthorne smiled and has been smiling ever since.

Victoria and Philip and Peony's coven met at Storm House, where they ate, drank, and were merry.

"Old Mather knew he was whupped," said Alfred P. Potsworth, dancing in a circle.

Jessica said, "Yes, people are not going to condone efforts to turn neighbor against neighbor in modern Salem -- unfortunately, though, the fires of judgmentalism and hate still burn."

Evelyn said, "We must keep channeling a spirit of tolerance and understanding. The Mathers' evil cannot prosper if people refuse to hate one another."

Philip said, "It would require a miracle for all the people on earth to understand one another."

"No. Just a little good magic," said Victoria. Moonbeam, sitting on her lap, began licking her face as if he were on a mission.

When the rest had departed, Philip stayed to help Victoria clean up. He asked whether Victoria was ready for a vacation after all the terrors of October.

"Oh, no, Philip," she answered, "I have to get my shop ready for Thanksgiving and Christmas. There are still several busy months ahead of us in Salem."

"Speaking of Thanksgiving, will you have dinner with my family? My parents are dying to meet you."

There was a different kind of magic in the air that night.

Away from Home
Gary Davis

I fly through gnarly oaks,
catching trills from screech-owls.

The animals know me.
They have that extra sense.

I commune with the crows,
like goddess Morrigan.

By day I sleep cozy,
hear few footsteps above.

Nighttime is when I reign,
amidst chirps and flutters.

Still, I'm always longing,
searching for that someplace.

I wish I were back home,
sound asleep in my bed,

instead of in this grave
for the unknown unmarked dead.

Self-Preservation
Lucretia Stanhope

Each desperate gulp of scalding coffee burned Angela's throat as she struggled to swallow the remnants of the greasy egg sandwich, clinging like a curse to her tongue.

It was a rare moment for one of the passing suits to extend anything beyond a snide remark, and she was determined to savor every crumb and drip before the fleeting charity dissipated.

The wide smiles of those around her resembled carnival masks, stretching beyond joy into the realm of the uncanny, their happiness a stark contrast to the weight of her own apprehension. Each gesture from the woman at the next table sent a wave of perfume, so floral it bordered on funerary, into the air, congealing with the aroma of burnt toast and sizzling bacon, forming a pungent stench.

Despite the gentle arch of the brows above the compassionate gaze of the man across from her, a shiver coursed through Angela. Years ago, when another generous man rescued her from her father's clutches, she learned that treats never came without bindings attached.

"There's something you can help me with," he said, his voice laden with implication.

Here it was, the inevitable cost of the sandwich now churning uncomfortably in her stomach, casting a shadow over the table like a dark omen amidst the bright facade of the café's atmosphere.

He pushed his plate forward, the pristine scrambled eggs and grits appearing more like a sacrificial offering than a gesture of kindness.

She paused with her fork suspended over the plate. "What's the catch?" The question emerged with a chilly tone she hadn't intended. Deep down, she knew she would consume the eggs and obediently follow him to whatever sleek car he had parked outside.

"My assistant left me in a bit of a bind. I need a replacement immediately." His gaze swept over Angela as if he were a painter searching for details to capture her. "It's for my wife."

Angela speared a bite of egg with her fork, noting the slip in his request. She wanted to inquire, "Is it for you or your wife?" but she held back, wary such astuteness might jeopardize her chance at a free meal. "I never graduated," she confessed instead.

His eyes lingered on her mouth as she chewed, and then he laughed. A sound so melodious it caught her off guard. "No experience necessary," he assured her with a smile.

Charming with all sharp lines and soulful eyes.

Mamma warned her, it was the pretty ones that had the ugliest hearts. She would have gone with him regardless.

As she devoured the remnants of the man's breakfast, the buzz of conversation around them faded into the background, replaced by the sound of his lyrical voice. He talked of urgency and desperation, his words dripping with honeyed promises and veiled intentions. His beloved wife, a formula in need of perfecting, time slipping away like grains of sand through an hourglass, and rewards for helping that sounded fantastical.

She could almost feel her mother's presence beside her, hand clasping hers tightly, voice whispering of deceit and betrayal. "Ain't no man going to give you more than he takes."

Surrounded by the cheerful bustle of the café, enveloped in the warmth of his promises, she made her choice. The allure of a warm bed, three meals a day, and the comfort of companionship beckoned like a siren's song, drowning out the warnings of her mother's voice.

Outside, cars raced past, their drivers oblivious as Angela slipped into the sleek, black Mercedes.

With a gentle click, he closed her door, drowning out the relentless symphony of self-absorbed hustle that served as the soundtrack to her existence.

In the stillness, she observed him glide gracefully around to the driver's side.

It wasn't the first Mercedes Angela rode in, but she always felt exposed as her dusty limbs brushed against the luxurious upholstery. However, it was the first time she found herself riding alongside such a striking man, amping the feeling up to vulnerable.

"Satan was the most beautiful angel," her mother often remarked.

After he started the car, locks clicked.

Her mouth dried.

Unnatural silence screamed at her, demanding to be filled.

"What's wrong with your wife?" She succumbed to the demand. Her voice tiny in the void of questions between them.

His thumb rubbed the steering wheel. "She's utterly perfect. It's the matter of time, you understand."

She didn't understand. Was he suggesting a perfect wife was a bad thing, or that his wife wasn't running out of time like he'd implied? "What's the formula for?"

"It's a matter of self-preservation." He cut his eyes toward her. "Do you know anything about Buddhists?"

"You mean the ones who meditate? Like with the crossed legs and all?" She picked at the dirt under a fingernail. "And can't have things."

"Crudely stated. It's a bit more complicated." Condescension soured his smooth voice.

What did that have to do with anything?

Answering her unspoken question, he enthused about monks who meditated themselves to a state of eternal life. The cityscape gave way to trees. While waxed on about Egyptians getting it wrong, shades of green zipped by in a blur, reminiscent of the oils in the art gallery windows by her favorite benches.

Scruffy and his shaggy dog named Here-Boy would probably enjoy the extra space on the benches while she was away helping... her thought stopped. "I'm Angela. What's your name?"

His sigh said he didn't appreciate being interrupted. "Angela."

It was odd the way he said her name. Like he found the taste of the letters disgusting and wanted to spit it out of his mouth and mind.

She fingered the doorhandle. He appeared nicer against the backdrop of the city.

"I'm very close to the perfect mixture," he continued, leaving her question unanswered. "It's down to the tree sap ratio."

The clack, clack of the turn signal played alongside his voice, alerting the emptiness behind them they'd be slowing.

"It's got to be from the inside out. That makes it tricky." He glanced at her in the sideways manner betters always did, as if looking at her straight on would dirty their eyes.

Pavement gave way to gravel before changing to dirt. Trees thickened, forming the illusion of a tunnel. The canopy above dimmed the light.

Angela imagined outside of the car the temperature dropped in that cool air way that clings to skin with eerie moisture. It probably smelled like fresh dirt, not like the dirt in the city.

The trees released their grip on Angela's thoughts, handing her over to a sight that clasped her attention like a vise.

A dilapidated structure loomed ahead, nestled within the opening. Its weather-worn brick exterior struggled to break free from the encroaching undergrowth. Third-floor windows, adorned with shattered glass, appeared as if nature itself were reclaiming the space, with vines creeping outward. Boards clumsily attempted to conceal the decay on the lower levels, yet failed to deter the curious gaze of birds peering through the gaps, their beady eyes fixated on the approaching car.

Angela's lungs refused to expand as she sucked in a breath. This was far from the picturesque manor she envisioned, where she might assist a devoted scientist in his quest to save his ailing wife. Nor was it the worst locale she found herself in with a companion. She knew better than to entertain the hope that this encounter might hold deeper significance. Even if it meant enduring a lengthy journey for mere moments of whatever he desired. "Where exactly have you brought us?"

"I require privacy for my work." He guided the car into a long-overgrown, circular drive before halting at the front door. "I've put my resources into the labs and supplies."

Was he really going to carry on with the pretense?

"We can do it in the car," she offered.

His expression twisted with disdain. "I assure you the car won't suffice. I did mention it will take weeks at least."

Did he? Why didn't she listen? Inside the building, in his car, or in the woods, it was up to him at this point. She gripped the handle.

Her mother would be pursing her lips, shaking her head, and saying, "One of these days if you don't pay attention, you'll pay with something else."

"I'll let you out," he said as he pocketed his keys.

Angela tried the handle a few times, finding it locked, before he opened her door.

He neglected to extend a hand to assist her as she exited the car, or to aid her in navigating the deteriorating concrete steps to the entrance.

Inside, the overhead lights flickered momentarily before settling on casting their harsh, overly bright glow down the hallway. Despite the decrepit exterior, the walls and floors within gleamed, as though meticulously polished by a team of maids. The air carried a sharp scent, reminiscent of bleach or some equally potent disinfectant.

She trailed behind him down the corridor until he halted at a door, unlocking it with a practiced motion.

"This is your room. I'm afraid for the sake of the project it needs to remain sterile." With a touch to the small of her back, he ushered her inside. The weight of his hand on her chilling her with an ominous sensation that lingered in the air. "There is a shower in the back. You'll find fresh clothes. I'll return with your lunch."

Angela nodded, words escaping her.

He closed the door, the decisive click of the knob indicating it was now locked.

Her gaze fixed on the barrier. Maybe he feared she'd wander around and ruin something or steal something of value. In the corner there was a small shower made of tiny while tiles. It reminded her of the showers from gym class. These weren't ugly pea green, like in her school, but shining as pretty as pearls. As she disrobed, her grungy clothes looked out of place on the clean linoleum floor that covered her room.

Occasionally she'd been taken to motels and asked to shower, so it wasn't totally unexpected. It was a pleasant change to be left alone to do it. Shampoo in a bottle he'd left on the floor in the shower failed to lather adequately on the initial attempt. Perhaps it was the shampoo's fault, but more likely it was because of the grime accumulated in her hair. It took until the third wash for the suds to finally emerge, providing a semblance of effectiveness, albeit with a scent reminiscent of laundry day. The soap shared the same fragrance. With the water running hot and her belly content, she didn't mind smelling like freshly laundered clothes if that was his preference.

What did he want from her? The thought nagged her. Most of them were clear before they gave her anything, or shortly thereafter. Could he really need her help with something important?

Images of free meals and warm nights trickled through her, soothing like the hot water rolling down her back. Feeling as clean as she had in months, she got out of the shower and dried off with a scratchy towel, using it under her feet once she was dry to mop up her mess.

The clothes he'd left were like the gown they made her wear when she'd been examined at the doctor's office. It even had the same strange laces in the back and on the shoulders. This one was prettier with little blue squares on the white material. The socks were a brighter blue than the gown, but she never matched anyway. That, and the odd rubber pattern on the bottom would keep her from slipping, assuming he didn't want her wearing her shoes on the clean floor.

She folded her clothes and placed them on the counter before walking to the bed and sitting down. There was nothing in the room to look at, so she picked at the bottom of the socks while she waited.

It felt like forever before he returned with a tray.

He lifted the lid, revealing a small paper cup and a marginally larger glass. His gaze rinsed over her. A soft tip at the edges of his mouth, the only sign he approved of her job at cleaning up.

Angela leaned over.

A blue pill with writing too small to read rested on the bottom of the paper cup. Sludgy liquid, the shade of coffee but looking more like the syrup on pancakes, halfway filled the glass.

Her nose scrunched. "I'm not hungry. If you want to do whatever, we can."

His knuckles gripped the tray so tight they turned white. "That's enough of that sort of talk. You said you would help me. Don't be a problem." He used a tone she knew well. One that meant you better obey if you didn't want a smack.

"Sure. Yes, sir." She stood. "Where are the files, or whatever?" Who said things couldn't be what they seem, and he just wanted her help?

"Self-preservation is achieved in both the body and mind." He flicked his gaze toward the pill. "That will grant you a meditative mind."

Angela chewed her lip. He was talking about the monk mummies again. "Me?"

The lift of his finely arched brows and the subtle tilt of his head conveyed his disbelief in her ability to meditate, mirroring her own doubts. "My wife shares your inattention to..." His voice trailed off as he paused, closed his eyes briefly, and shook his head. "Take the pill."

As she lifted the cup from the tray, she noticed the weight, surprisingly heavy for a mere paper cup. Memories flooded her mind of the last time she took a pill from one of them. Awakening disoriented and damp beneath a bush in the nearby park. "What's in the syrup?"

"I explained that already." Frustration wrenched the handsome from his face. "I don't have time to repeat myself."

The pill hesitated in the back of her mouth, leaving behind a faint chemical trail as it crept down her throat.

"There we are." His demeanor softened. A charming smile illuminated his features as he handed her the glass. "All of it."

As if trying to outdo the pill, the drink threatened to come back up with each sip.

He watched until she emptied every thick drop. His eyes locked on her with a deeper fascination. "Tell me everything you feel."

"Warm. Everything feels warm." Her words danced in the air, stretching and warping as if they were alive and no longer belonged to her.

The sound of his pen scraping against the tablet reverberated like beetles attempting to escape from a tomb.

Time turned inside out as she talked, and he captured her words.

"Meditate. I'll return with your dinner." He guided her to lie down with a gentleness that made her feel cherished, as if she were his most precious possession. No one had ever touched her in such a tender manner, not even her mamma.

Days blurred together as he brought more and more of the sludgy liquid. The pills ceased, and he assured her that her mind was now calm.

Angela knew better. Without the pills, her thoughts raged like tempestuous storms in the spring. How long had she been here? Why couldn't she move or feel the familiar touch of the stethoscope against her chest? Most alarming of all was her inability to make a sound, not even a whimper to let him know that she was not peacefully meditating. This was not tranquility.

More days passed. Was it weeks yet?

She couldn't swallow, so he inserted something into her arm attached to bags of the slush that he'd hung beside her bed.

"I'm not relaxed. Please." She wanted to scream, but the words were imprisoned by her own voiceless existence.

He frowned down at her before throwing his stethoscope across the room. "Not again," he shouted and paced beside the edge of her bed. "Why?"

Footsteps leaving.

The door didn't close with the usual click.

Silence.

Rattling, like the sound a shopping cart makes when two of the wheels don't quite work right, neared.

"Have to start all over again," he muttered as he tossed her from the bed to a cold metal cart.

She stared up, unable to move, as he pushed her down the hallway.

The overhead lights glared down at her as if they, too, were disappointed in her performance.

Angela listened as all the things he'd said while administering her drinks replayed. Living mummies. Self-made. "I'm alive."

The cart came to a stop and fresh air surrounded her.

Everything bucked like a roller-coaster ride.

Above, the night encased the sky.

"At this rate I'll need another pit." He sneered down at her. "So promising."

"It worked! It worked! Please. I'm alive," she screamed in her mind. Her mouth remained motionless. Not even a breath escaped her lips.

Angela's body plunged straight down into the pit. Her eyes refused to close despite her efforts. The remains of those before her, tossed haphazardly on top of the other, grew clear as she plummeted toward the pit's bottom.

A crunching thud reverberated as she collided with the corpses below.

There was no stench of decay. Not even the odor you notice when walking down the meat aisle in the grocery store. Just an odd mix of the smell pine needles leave on your hands when you braid them to make friendship bracelets mixed with the smell of a room where someone who was sick is resting.

As her vision adjusted to the dark, open eyes stared back at her. Blue with a yellowed tinge in the whites.

"Are you alive?" The question looped in Angela's thoughts, allowing her to avoid the horror of the answer to the question lurking in the shadows of her mind. The question she should have asked before drinking the formula.

"What happens if it works?" A question she wished she asked.

The fate of his self-preserved mummies hinged on their longevity.

Time warped as she pondered the possibilities.

A dashing hero would chance upon the pit, accompanied by a team of esteemed archaeologists who would delicately unearth the remains. These artifacts would then embark on a journey, showcased in a prestigious traveling museum exhibition, reminiscent of the displays she had admired through the windows she once slept beneath.

But now, transformed from discarded waste to a globally treasured artifact, she would find solace in the warmth indoors.

An eternally preserved reminder of the consequences of not paying attention.

Hallows' Eve
Allison Liu

The trees reach with withered fingers
For the pale moon,
Her weary light veiled in shadowed sky.
Within swirls of mist, among curtains and clotheslines,
Ghosts come alive to haunt us.

The air cools.
At the wind's whispering,
Leaves like flecks of dried blood
Drift listlessly to the ground,
Corpses awaiting the shroud of snow.

Dark clouds portend grim fortunes
As we bundle up against the coming cold—
Hats placed on small heads,
Scarves wrapped tight around necks,
Like nooses hoisting those who would rise on this day.

For a single night,
Heads grin menacingly from the pumpkin fields,
And glasses fill with blood.
The widow and her black bombay,
A witch and her familiar.

By morning's light we rake the windswept leaves,
Pull down dry dresses and sheets,
Look to the clouds in search of showers,
Ghouls of yesterday
Forgotten.

Haunted

K. S. Hardy

The dust
Of my grave
Absorbs my tears
My dearly beloved
Did not love
Me dearly,
Yet he will not
Get away with it.
I will chew at
His heart with fear.
I will poison
His mind with dreams.
I will haunt
Him to confession.
Then through the floor door
They will drop him
To dangle at rope end
And he will be mine again,
Buried beside me forever.

The Haunting of Loon Lake
Tom Folske

Tessa Nells, her brother Teron, Teron's girlfriend Victoria Shep, and Tessa's best friend Maxwell Howser, were all amateur ghost hunters. Their group, The Haunt Hunters, was well received both locally and on the web, with almost ten thousand subscribers, and they had been all over Minnesota, exploring every haunted location they could gain access to. The group had investigated the Glensheen Mansion, Smiling Jack in the Roselawn Cemetery, the Ramsey County Courthouse, the old Hamm Mansion, the abandoned Tunnel of Terror, even the Dog-Man in Otter Tail County, and now it was time for them to do a show on the incredibly haunted Loon Lake Cemetery.

"The Loon Lake Cemetery is especially creepy for myriad reasons," Tessa started, speaking into the camera. "The first and most obvious of which is the fact that loons themselves are psychopomps, guides to the dearly departed, and their cries are eerie enough to send a shiver down your spine, even on the clearest of nights. The second reason as to why this haunted location is especially scary, is because of the simple fact that it's an old, abandoned cemetery. This will be the second cemetery The Haunt Hunters have visited for the show, the first being the Roselawn Cemetery for Smiling Jack, but this time, we intend to spend the night out there and livestream the whole thing. Now, the third, and most important thing that makes this place truly terrifying, is the tragic event that occurred here back in 1880.

"It all started when a young girl named Mary Jane Terwillegar was suspected of being a witch. The legend goes that on March 5th, 1880, Mary, and two other women, her alleged coven, were captured by the townsfolk of nearby Petersburg, Minnesota. It is said they were caught in the middle of performing an occult ritual in which all three girls, for they were girls, not a single one of them was over the age of eighteen, were covered in the blood of several recently dismembered black cats. They were in the process of slitting the throat of a goat.

"The authorities or the church, it is unclear which, then basically broke in, violently rounded up all three girls, and without trial, brought them into the cemetery to be burnt at the stake. Fortunately for the girls, I suppose, the townsfolk were unable to get the pyre together in time, and fearing they would not be able to hold Mary Jane much longer, they made a rash decision. The reverend, for the legend is clear it was the reverend and not the sheriff, grabbed the sharpest axe he could procure, and had each girl kneel over a stump. He then proceeded to behead them one at a time.

"He allegedly beheaded Mary Jane's coven first, before turning his axe on the supposed head witch herself, who until that moment had remained silent, a scornful scowl on her face as she helplessly watched the brutal deaths of her sisters. "You can kill me," Mary Jane allegedly told the reverend quietly, emotionlessly, "But I did make a deal with The Fallen One. Sixty-six souls, reverend. I need to feed sixty-six souls to what lurks in the infernal pits before I can return, and yours will be the first." Mary Jane then returned to silence. When the reverend attempted to behead her, she refused to be turned around. The strength of three grown men could not make her turn, so the reverend was left with no choice but to decapitate the young girl while she stared with utter malice, directly into his eyes.

"The rest of the legend states that Mary Jane's head rolled away from her body, but her eyes never left those of the reverend. He died of a heart attack right there on the spot," Tessa finished her opening monologue that she had been practicing every day, multiple times a day for the last two weeks.

Viewership had jumped up to almost twelve thousand during Tessa's intro, which is the largest number of views the show had ever received, and they weren't even in the cemetery yet. Thankfully, the group had learned from past mistakes, and had actually gone to the Petersburg city council, being that the Loon Lake cemetery was, for all intents and purposes, abandoned, and because they actually went through the proper channels, unlike so many who had come before them, the city council pretty much gave them free range to do as they pleased, essentially telling them they wouldn't be bothered as long as they weren't loud or out there destroying stuff. The group didn't, however, mention that they were going to be performing a séance.

Tessa stepped out of the car as Maxwell continued to film and Teron continued to direct. Victoria was mostly on lighting and sometimes sound, but she was also acting as a go'fer for the rest of them. As they entered the cemetery, Maxwell and Teron constantly adjusted the camera to find the perfect shot as they prepped for Tessa to cross over the threshold. It was a slow start, with Tessa basically making small comments on the spookiest looking tombstones or questioning where the decapitations could have taken place, hoping to create a spooky atmosphere and ambience, but knowing that things couldn't be truly scary until it was full dark. Right now, it was only mid-dusk.

The show kept viewers for a while, then they started to drop off rapidly until nightfall, when they started to rise again, concurrently with the darkness. Being as they were so far away from any other people, and although it was a clear night, with a full moon (best for viewership), and practically all the stars in the sky were showing, illuminating every headstone in the vicinity, it was an utterly strange experience. They could see all around them clearly, but the night also made them feel completely isolated, like the stars were small teeth and the night sky had swallowed everyone up in its gaping maw.

The viewership stayed stable, only increasing a little when they thought they heard or saw something, and slacking a little if they went too long without hearing or seeing anything. This was pretty much what they had expected to happen. Around eleven o'clock, after they had done a walkthrough, exploring most of the cemetery for the viewers, they returned to the spot Teron and Maxwell had earlier deemed the spookiest locale in the whole cemetery. It was a secluded area on a slight hillock, near a small, round patch of blackened grass that looked like it had been burnt. Tessa had the spur of the moment idea to tell the audience that it was the spot where Mary Jane's head had landed, and that the grass hadn't grown there since.

Viewership began to steadily increase as it grew closer to midnight, as Teron and Victoria started to set up for the séance, the projected highlight of the show.

At 11:58 p.m. The Haunt Hunters all stood around a collapsible table they had brought from the car, holding hands, with the camera on a tripod recording their every movement.

At 11:59 p.m., Tessa Nells spoke these words: "Mary Jane, Mary Jane Terwillegar. We request your presence. Please make contact here tonight. We know you were wronged. We are sorry. We want to apologize. We just want to hear your side of the story."

At 12:00, nothing happened.

At 12:01, the blurry image of a girl appeared briefly in the frame for just a moment, before the camera cut out completely, abruptly ending The Haunt Hunters' live feed and leaving many viewers frustrated, terrified, or both.

Tessa was the first to see the spectral girl, and to see through her as well. She broke the connection and stumbled away from the table as everyone else turned to see what she was looking at.

Even if they hadn't been in a cemetery, even if it hadn't been midnight, and the girl hadn't been dirty and semi-translucent, the expression Mary Jane Terwillegar wore on her face was once of pure lunacy. If seen in the wild, her eyes alone could have made the bravest of men tremble. Teron and Maxwell, both scared out of their wits, both still managed to make sure the girls were behind them as the ghastly figure approached, floating leisurely toward them, her downward pointed toes inches off the ground.

"Run," Teron yelled at the girls as he lunged toward the oncoming menace. The figure grabbed him by the throat before he could attack, and when Maxwell went to help with a haymaker, he was grabbed by a second woman, just as ethereal as the first. Tessa and Victoria turned in unison and burst away from the scene. Tessa had been a sprinter in high school and unfortunately for Victoria, it showed. Victoria was grabbed by a third, horrid, ghostly figure as Tessa continued to run on into the night, watching as the ghost of Mary Jane Terwillegar began to rip her brother's skin from his body in long, wet, thick strips.

Tessa continued to run as she witnessed the look of unfathomable fear in both Maxwell and Victoria's eyes as the other two witches began to de-flesh most of the remaining Haunt Hunters. Victoria reached out to Tessa as her face was torn away from her skull, mid-plea, exposing eyeballs suddenly loose in their sockets and revealing a lipless top row of teeth. Tessa couldn't help but burst into tears.

Unfortunately, because she was looking backward and not forward, Tessa ran into and literally flipped over a tombstone, instantly knocking the wind out of herself, and sending a shooting pain up her spine. Tessa could hear the wild cackling encroaching upon her, however, and even though she couldn't breathe, she knew she had to get up, she had to keep going. Tessa forced herself into a breathless, stumbling jog as she advanced further into the graveyard, not daring to look back as she expected that any minute, one of the witches' gnarled hands would grasp her up off her feet and drag her into the darkness.

It wasn't until she started physically gagging, when her lungs felt like she was inhaling embers, that Tessa finally had to stop, pausing to catch her breath against a statue of the Virgin Mary. Thankfully, she could no longer hear the mad cackling following her. Tessa then actually did throw up, and was about to finish on with her escape, when she looked up and screamed.

Surrounding her in every direction, were myriad phantoms and specters, all dressed in their archaic death garments, and all with covetous grimaces upon their abhorrent visages. Tessa could feel their yearning, their jealousy for that which they could never again obtain, their cacoethes for life. The spirits all floated inches off the ground as they slowly encroached, staring at Tessa with ravenous expectation.

Tessa crouched back down, knowing she couldn't waste the time, but feeling she had to perform what could potentially be her one final act anyway. She quickly fumbled her phone out of her too-tight pocket, twisting her leg to do so, and instead of calling the cops, which at this point she realized would be entirely futile anyway, Tessa opened the app that connected her to the Haunt Hunters' live feed, the feature Teron had all of them add to their phones, in case they ever saw something scary when the cameras weren't rolling.

"I love you Mom and Dad. I'm so sorry for all the times I hurt you. Teron too. Goodbye," Tessa cried dismally into the screen.

Tessa then stood up and bolted through the converging dead, narrowly avoiding their grasps as she ran, screaming and crying, in the direction of the cemetery's front gate. She made it over half the distance, dropping her phone somewhere along the way, and for a moment, Tessa thought, hoped she was going to make it the whole way out, but just when the entrance was in sight, she felt cold, earth-dampened hands close around her ankles, tripping her to the ground, before those same, wet, brackish hands clasped onto her wrists.

There was no video, Tessa's phone had landed facedown when she had dropped it, but anyone who still happened to be tuned into the Haunt Hunters' live feed, heard as Tessa struggled toward safety, toward hope, but was instead weighed down by the countless dead as she was plunged into an odious, voracious darkness, into the demented, sadistic cackling and callous, inhuman embrace of malevolent pandemonium.

Who?

Lucretia Stanhope, a relentlessly optimistic chronic illness warrior with less grace than determination, navigates her crone stage in a quaint Midwest town surrounded by cornfields. Amidst enduring medical trials that could rival horror stories, her pen never rests. From crafting heart-melting romances to spine-tingling horrors, she weaves tales as intricately as she crochets yarn. When not lost in the wonderful lands of her imagination, she finds solace in doting on her two chihuahuas and her endlessly patient husband, a fellow scribe who shares her love for storytelling, boundless enthusiasm for the adventures yet to unfold, and never denies her dessert first.

Christopher Langan is a science fiction writer who is enamored with the process of creating entire worlds filled with larger than life characters. He marvels at how such an amazing feat could be accomplished by a three-pound cluster of cells that drives a skeleton. He believes that flowery literature is amazing but relishes the art of presenting an engaging story in its simplest form.

Greg Schwartz says: Since the pandemic I've been working from my basement. When time and my children allow, I try to write. Other than Illumen, Some of my poems have been published in Scifaikuest, Space & Time, Abyss & Apex, and Utopia Science Fiction.

Tom Folske lives in Minnesota with his wife, soon to be five kids, and three black cats. He holds a BA in creative writing and has been creating stories for over two decades. He has had or is in the process of having over 20 short stories published. Tom loves horror in all forms, especially 80's and 90's horror, and is a comic nerd, a cinephile, an audiobook junkie, a horror buff, and above all things, a storyteller.

Paul Lonardo is a freelance writer and author with numerous titles, both fiction and nonfiction books. He's placed short fiction and nonfiction articles in various genre magazines and ezines. He is a contributing writer for Tales from the Moonlit Path and an active HWA member.

Katherine Kerestman is the author of Lethal (PsychoToxin Press, 2023) and Creepy Cat's Macabre Travels: Prowling around Haunted Towers, Crumbling Castles, and Ghoulish Graveyards (WordCrafts Press, 2020), as well as the co-editor (with S. T. Joshi) of The Weird Cat, an anthology of weird cat stories by writers living and dead (WordCrafts Press, October 2023). Her Lovecraftian and gothic works have been featured in Black Wings VII, Penumbra, Journ-E, Spectral Realms, Illumen, Retro-Fan and The Little Book of Cursed Dolls (Media Macabre, 2023), as well as other discerning publications. Katherine is wild about Dark Shadows and Twin Peaks. When she is not cavorting in the graveyards of Salem on

Halloween, you can find her worshipping with the Cult of Cthulhu at the H. P. Lovecraft Film Festival. She may be stalked at www.creepycatlair.com.

Poet Laureate of New Bedford, Massachusetts from 2014 to 2021, author and playwright **Patricia Gomes** is published in numerous literary journals and anthologies. Gomes is the author of four poetry chapbooks. Her interest in horror began with a childhood obsession with Fate Magazine, countless Hammer Films Horror Classics, and all things Vincent Price. Some call her twisted; most call her Gomesie.

Gary Davis enjoys exercising his imagination through crafting dark and darkly humorous poems and stories. He particularly likes classic supernatural horror topics. In poetry, imagery of the senses is important. Poetry is a form of painting within Japanese Zen. In an anthology such as Potter's Field, it is also important to convey a sense of the loneliness of the unmarked grave within a vast universe.

Lee Clark Zumpe, an entertainment editor with Tampa Bay Newspapers, earned his bachelor's in English at the University of South Florida. He began writing poetry and fiction in the early 1990s. His work has regularly appeared in a variety of literary journals and genre magazines over the last two decades.

Lee's inclination toward horror manifested itself early in his childhood when he began flipping through the pages of Forrest J. Ackerman's *Famous Monsters of Filmland* and reading Gold Key Comic classics like *Boris Karloff Tales of Mystery* and *Grimm's Ghost Stories*. In his teenage years, he discovered Edgar Allan Poe, H.P. Lovecraft, Ambrose Bierce, Richard Matheson and other masters of the genre. Lee's work often focuses on character interaction set against a pervading sense of cosmic dread and high strangeness.

Lee lives on the west coast of Florida with his wife and daughter.

www.ingramcontent.com/pod-product-compliance
Lightning Source LLC
LaVergne TN
LVHW021222080526
838199LV00089B/5788